M000312307

Bliss

THE FREED BILLIONAIRE
SPENCER CHRISTMAS TRILOGY
BOOK THREE

Z.L. ARKADIE

Copyright © 2019 by Z. L. Arkadie

All rights reserved.

No part of this book may be reproduced in any form or by any electronic or mechanical means, including information storage and retrieval systems, without written permission from the author, except for the use of brief quotations in a book review.

ISBN: 978-1-942857-76-1

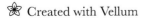 Created with Vellum

CHAPTER ONE

JADA FORTE

After ending my call with my dad, I texted Spencer to inform him I was on my way to the hospital, determined to have it out with my mother.

Wait. I'll go with you, he texted back.

I responded by turning off my phone. My mom and I had family business to discuss. It would be her and me, and she would answer for what I had found in her closet. I was certain Spencer could understand that, since my mom had known about his father's atrocious acts and, instead of turning him into the authorities, she used what she'd learned to her advantage.

I strolled right by the lobby and reporters, who were finally contained by hospital administration.

They yelled at me from a restricted location, but none approached. I was glad they saw me, though. Deep down, I was a little afraid of a person who would stoop to levels my mother had. I was out of the fold, no longer her congenital disciple.

Earlier, while pulled over to the side of the road, bawling my eyes out, my dad had called. He'd pled with me to talk to my mother.

"She framed Stefan," he'd said.

I could hardly believe what my father claimed. "Stefan Rothschild, your son?"

"Yes, and he's your brother. Your mother has let her job go to her fucking head. She's not the same woman I married. Only you can get to her."

I'd blinked my eyes hard, trying to make sense of what my father was saying. I felt as if I were fully awake yet trapped in a nightmare.

I shook my head like a rattle. "But I don't understand. How did mom frame…" I didn't know what to call him. Should I refer to him as my father's son? My brother? "Stefan?" I asked, settling on defining him in a way where he didn't belong to me or my father.

My phone had beeped as my dad began his explanation. I saw the caller was Spencer, and even though I had a lot to say to my lover, I didn't want to interrupt my dad to take his call.

Apparently, my mother had invited Stefan to her home to meet me. Stefan had heard a lot about me and wanted to finally meet me in person. He drove all the way from Los Angeles to Santa Barbara and, after arriving, hadn't taken many steps away from his car before someone put a rag over his face. He'd kicked, elbowed, and tried to wriggle out of a strong man's grasp, but slowly, dizziness gave way to unconsciousness. When he came to, he was propped up against his car, head fuzzy and everything around him feeling still and undisturbed. For a moment, he thought he had hallucinated the attack but felt the throbbing of aches and pangs.

When he'd gathered his bearings enough to stagger to the front door, he rang the doorbell. No one answered. After trying for a while, he got back in his car and went home, determined to put the odd experience behind him. Yesterday, two detectives showed up at his apartment on the beach in Santa Monica and brought him to the station for questioning. They hadn't charged him with a crime yet but had been questioning him about the shooting, trying to convince Stefan to confess to being responsible for it.

"I know Pat set him up. I know because the department is giving my lawyer shit, telling him Stefan is lost in the system, but I know what they're doing. The only way charges will stick is if he confesses. Those crooked assholes are trying to put pressure. I swear I'll sue that fucking department if they lay a hand on my son."

The account was harrowing, and before I had found the documents in her closet, I may have been more inclined to question my father's claim. However, I now knew what my mother was capable of. I had to ask him a few more questions before trusting him completely.

"What about my phone?" I'd asked.

"What?" He sounded impatient and clueless.

"Someone made it so that my phone wouldn't accept calls from Spencer, and his mine. Did you help Mom do that?"

"No. I would never agree to do that. And your mother doesn't need me to do her dirty work. She has a network of sycophants for that." I pictured him shaking his head swiftly before saying, "Just talk to her, okay? Get her to call this charade off right now."

I had gone from crying to feeling shaky as I changed course. Instead of heading to the airport to fly back to New York, I drove to the hospital. Dad still believed I had power to sway my mother. I wondered if he was right. If she loved me, would she work so hard to control me?

Before I made it to the check-in desk, one of the men waved me toward the elevator.

As I rode up to the floor my mother's room was on, I made a pact with myself. There was no time to pussyfoot around. I had to get to the point and make my mom answer for her schemes. I wondered if I should mention what I'd found in her closet. If I released those pages to the public, her career would be ruined. The fact that she knew of Randolph Christmas's repulsive acts against young girls and kept it quiet by extorting him for money made me clutch my stomach and breathe through my nausea.

And to write the word "hush" on the back of one of the pages? Evil. My mom couldn't deny it was her who wrote it. I knew her handwriting. She had written it.

The elevator doors slid open. I took strong, purposeful steps toward my mom's room. Her security guard, Clinton, wasn't standing outside her door. He had been replaced with another one named Hugh. I made a quick approach, intending to walk right through his burly frame if he didn't step aside.

"Jada, how are you?" Hugh asked, his tone as dry as his facial expression.

"I'm fine, thanks." He was used to me inquiring about his well-being, but at that moment, I saw anyone tasked with protecting my mother as the enemy.

I pushed the hospital room door open, and the sight of my mom's team seated around her bed made me stop abruptly.

I leaned back and checked my watch to make sure it was actually as late as I'd thought it was. "Yeah, it's after midnight."

"Jada?" my mom asked, appearing genuinely surprised to see me.

Apparently, she knew I had left the hospital. My chest tightened. I wondered if she knew I went to her house.

"You seemed just as shocked to see me as I am to see your team. You said you were keeping them safe at home. What changed? Did they catch the shooter?"

All eyes were on me, and the tension settling in the air couldn't be sliced with a chainsaw. Danny,

Serena, Foster, May, and Chris had never heard me take such a cynical tone with my mother, and I was sure it was why they were looking at me with such intrigue.

My mom closed her laptop, which, despite her gunshot wound, she had done without wincing.

"Leave me alone with my daughter," she said.

I hated her tone. It made me feel as if she had just shaved twenty years off my life. I reminded myself to stay strong and not fold as her staff passed me on their way out. None of them made eye contact with me as I kept my glare fastened on my mother's face.

Once we were alone, she grinned as she positioned herself comfortably and crossed her arms on her chest. "I thought you ran off to be with that Christmas boy."

I was still processing the fact that she had just insulted Spencer by referring to him as a "boy" when her eyes suddenly expanded, and she pressed her hand over her heart.

"Haven't you heard? It was your brother who shot me, and he wants to do the same to you."

I hadn't realized until that very moment that I had been shaking my head, unable to stop. A lot had changed about the way I listened to her though, since I'd lost all trust in her. First, my father had told me Stefan hadn't been booked, only questioned. The fact she mentioned it was her way of testing whether I'd heard from my dad. And I figured I hadn't bolted into her room to sugarcoat things. There was no time like the present to get to the point.

"Mom, did you frame Stefan for shooting you?" I asked.

Her smirk grew more intense, cynical. "Stefan? Is that what you're calling him now?"

"Dad said you called Stefan over to your house after telling him I wanted to meet him and that you would host our get-together. Is that true?" I studied her closely.

There was the pause. I'd expected her to pause because I'd expected her to lie.

"No, it is not true," she claimed.

I shook my head again. "Stop this, Mom."

Her brows raised slightly. "Stop what?"

I sighed. It was clear I wasn't making any headway with her at all. There was something I wasn't understanding. The longer I looked at the dare in her eyes and the claim of victory on her lips, the closer to illumination I arrived. My mom actually believed I trusted her, that no matter what, she could convince me to stand by her side.

Why wouldn't she believe that? I had fallen for every single one of her manipulations. My friends could see through her more clearly than I had. So many times Hope had tried to convince me it wasn't healthy to ditch and dodge my mother, only for me to go leaping to Patricia's whim whenever she'd crafted the right kind of story that sent me back to living under her thumb. I had never grasped even a kernel of what Hope meant until now. The payoff for my mom was convincing me to eventually drop my defenses and say yes to whatever she asked of me. And I felt free as long as I was running from her. However, I always knew she was right behind me, breathing down my neck, and soon I would be in her clutches. As I stood looking into the face of the woman I loved so much, I made a vow to stop the cycle in its tracks. I slipped my hand into my jacket pocket and touched the papers I'd found in her closet.

My mom patted the side of her bed, gesturing for me to sit beside her. "Jada, come, sit."

My feet remained planted to the ground. No more avoidance. It was time to get down to business. "Mom, how well did you know Randolph Christmas?"

She stiffened and then lifted her hand off the mattress. "What did you say?"

I cleared my throat and pulled my shoulders back, standing a hair taller. "Randolph Christmas, how well did you know him?"

Her eyes narrowed to slits, and I instantly knew what that look on her face meant. Not only was she unhappy with me but I was very close to being punished for my insolence. Regardless, I dug deep, reminding myself I was no longer a child. I was confronting my mother, adult to adult. So, I made sure to show no signs of weakness.

"You didn't answer my question, Mom. Did you know Randolph Christmas on a personal or professional level?"

Her lips parted but then she pursed them.

I raised a finger in warning. "And if I were you, I wouldn't lie this time."

She readjusted herself in her comfortable-looking hospital bed. "What do you think you know about Randolph and me?"

My head was spinning, my skin hot, and my eyes seeing red. "Here's what I know. You knew he was a pedophile, and instead of turning him into the authorities, you extorted him for money."

Her head fell back, and she laughed as if what I'd said was the funniest thing she'd ever heard.

I watched her, like a hawk waiting for her prey to come out of a hole in the ground, keeping my eyes narrowed, jaw set, unwilling to be detoured from my accusation. I knew the truth, and I wanted her to admit her wrongdoing.

"Who told you that, Randolph's son? A man who comes from the caliber of human being that Randolph was? Trash, who thank goodness is dead and buried in his fucking grave."

I closed my eyes and released a very slow breath. My skin crawled. My chest wanted to explode. "Mom, please tell the truth."

She folded her arms. "I don't know what you think you know, but I'm not going to confess to something I didn't do. I'm wondering if I can trust you. Has your boyfriend brainwashed you against me?"

I couldn't stand it anymore. I reached into my pocket and pulled out the papers. "Isn't this your handwriting?" I asked, holding them up so she could see the back of one of the pages in which she wrote "hush for girls."

Her eyes tapered as she garnered a good look at what I was showing her. Her head turned slightly, then she calmly sat back against the bed. "Where did you get that?"

"Did you blackmail Randolph Christmas to stay quiet about what you knew?"

If looks could kill, I would've been buried six feet under. That meant I was getting to her, and since I had her on the ropes, I figured I'd keep punching.

"Whatever you're doing to Stefan, stop, or else I'm turning these over to the press."

It happened in slow motion as far as my eyes could perceive. My mom reached for something on the table. She pressed a button. The door opened. In walked Hugh, who was towering behind me.

"Yes, Senator," he said.

"Um…" She twisted to get one of her pillows and then beat on it to fluff it. "Jada has some papers she's going to hand over to you. Also, she's not going to leave this hospital."

She spoke with a calm sense of assurance that all she requested would come to fruition.

I gauged the distance between where I stood and the door. If I said nothing and just ran, I could probably make it out. Once I was out of the room, I could start screaming. If I made a scene, my mom would back off. That, I was sure of.

My brain was in overdrive, and my feet must've taken some steps because the next thing I knew, I heard my mother say, "Stop her and get those papers."

I was trying to stuff them back in my pocket, but Hugh had his hands on me. There was no way I could compete with his strength, but I was going to use all of mine to get the hell out of my mother's room and take the papers with me.

Hugh's rock-hard chest hit against my shoulder, and his big hands wrapped around my wrist. Even when I elbowed him in the ribs, I knew I was fighting a losing battle.

"No, stop," I whimpered, focused on the pages in my hand, strangely afraid of harming them.

"Let Hugh have them, Jada," I heard my mom say.

I was able to bite his bicep, and as a result, he pushed me down. When I hit the floor, I was no longer holding the papers. The sting of my body slamming against the linoleum made me grunt and wince. But still, I wasn't done fighting. When I looked up at Hugh, I thought I was seeing an apparition of Spencer, who had his forearm against Hugh's windpipe and was squeezing.

Hugh tried different tactics to release himself, including trying to elbow Spencer in the ribs, but Spencer had been ready for it. The two large men were wrestling. When their bodies hit the floor, Spencer still had his arm around Hugh's throat and was telling him to release the papers or he'd die.

Hugh threw the papers out of his hand and I jumped on them, retrieving them.

"Stop! Nurse, nurse!" my mom called.

"Jada, get out of the room and leave the door open," Spencer ordered, his voice dwarfing my mom's.

My gaze bounced from him keeping Hugh immobilized to my mother. I didn't want to leave Spencer alone with both of them.

"Jada, move now!" Spencer shouted.

"Jada, don't go anywhere," my mom barked.

She was out of the bed and heading toward me. I didn't want her to touch me. My feet started moving, and with each rapid step, I made sure not to forget Spencer's instructions. I knew why leaving the door open was important. It was the same reason Jimmy had always behaved like everybody's favorite person at donor events. Everyone who worked at the hospital was a voter, and it behooved my mother to constantly convince them she was worth their vote.

I flung the door open, and a nurse who was walking toward the room stopped in her tracks. At first, she frowned curiously at the two men on the floor. Then Spencer let go of Hugh and rolled smoothly to his feet. He backed out of the room and then put his arm around me, making me feel protected.

"Is everything okay?" the nurse shrieked from the hallway. She was definitely being cautious, keeping a healthy amount of distance from Spencer and Hugh. Hugh was slowly rising to his feet, coughing to get his breaths back.

"Irina Petrov," my mom said loud enough so we could hear but not the nurse.

Spencer stiffened and watched my mother with a glare so cold it could freeze the sun.

"A fourteen-year-old boy. Prostitutes. Your father watching. Don't tempt me to parade those girls in front of a camera and let them tell the world how they experienced you."

I gasped, shaking my head. My mom's entire expression transformed from wickedness to astonishment. I realized she didn't know I knew about that part of Spencer's past, and now she did. To bring that up… To throw such a horrible experience in Spencer's face…

"Let's go, Jada," Spencer said.

My head felt floaty as he turned me away from my mother, who still watched me with her lips parted. She knew. I knew. She and I were at the point of no return. I would never see her the same. I would have to love her the way I saw her now or never love her again.

CHAPTER TWO

JADA FORTE

nother nurse arrived on the scene, eyeing us suspiciously as she entered my mom's room on the heels of the first nurse. Their voices speaking in exclamations became more distant as we made our way up the hallway.

I was hopped up on adrenaline. When we stood in front of the elevator, waiting for it to open, Spencer took me by my shoulders and turned me to face him.

"Are you hurt?" he asked, his glare roaming my face.

I squeezed my eyes shut, trying to stop the last thing my mom said to him from replaying in my head like an audio loop.

"I'm sorry my mom said those things," I whispered.

"I asked if you're hurt," he said curtly.

I felt my pensive expression. The answer to his question wasn't so cut and dry. My heart hurt, and I was sure I would never be able to rid myself of the picture of my mom standing there, saying those horrible things to Spencer.

"Because if you are..." He turned his glower toward the corridor we had just abandoned. "I'll kill him."

"I'm fine," I said in a rush.

His eyebrows pulled some, as if he needed more convincing.

"Only my front teeth ache from biting his bicep, but that's it."

The elevator doors slid open, and I found myself tugging Spencer into the car. We needed to put some serious distance between him, my mom, and Hugh. I could feel the fury coming off Spencer's body like smoke out of a chimney.

I examined our reflections on the silver panel in front of us. My hair was messy with strands freed from my loose ponytail, and my cheeks burned red. Spencer's face was pinched by so much anger it appeared as if he'd never find relief.

"As I said, I'm sorry about what my mom said."

"Jada, don't apologize for your mother's words and deeds," he said, continuing to look straight ahead.

"I'm just…" I closed my eyes to sigh gravely. When I opened my eyes, he was scrutinizing me. "Embarrassed," I managed to whisper.

The seconds slipped by, and I wondered what he was thinking. I had to think of something to say, so I blurted the first thing that came to my head. "You really kicked Hugh's ass."

His frown remained intense. "I can fight, but I don't like doing it. And I would've never had to if you hadn't decided to come here alone. I wanted you to wait for me, Jada."

I pressed my lips, scowling at the floor. "I guess I wanted her to come clean. I knew I had a better chance of that if I came alone."

Spencer scoffed. Suddenly his face was close to mine. I moved rearward until my back was pressed against the wall.

"Do you think Randolph Christmas would've ever come clean?" he asked.

I gulped and my lips remained pasted together. I felt as if he were asking me because he wanted me to say that my mother was no Randolph Christmas so he could laugh bitterly and dismiss me as a naïve woman. I wished I could defend my mother. Twenty-four hours ago, I would've, but she had shown me the part of herself that was indefensible.

"Your mother is never coming clean, Jada. Do you get that?"

I nodded, acquiescing.

"And those papers that almost got you killed while trying to protect them? You didn't need them." He positioned himself beside me. "I have what I need to prove the tie between Patricia and Randolph."

He didn't say "your mother and my father," and I guessed it was because he wanted to take the personal connections out of taking down my mother. Something very close to my surface wanted to fight for her, beg him to give her a chance to see the light. But that smirk on her mouth... She tried to have Hugh apprehend me. And then that fatal ending before our departure murdered the last kernel of respect I'd had for her.

"You never told me, who's Irina Petrov?"

Spencer's stare penetrated my reflection in the silver panel just as the doors slid open. He held out an arm to keep the door open. "Ladies first," he said.

I hesitated. Once again, he was choosing to not answer me. Two people were waiting to enter the elevator, so I decided against not moving an inch until he told me who she was. My feet were as light as air as I stepped onto the linoleum. Spencer rushed out behind me, and we headed toward the lobby.

"I want you to drive to the airport and return your car. I'll have an airplane take you to a secure location. It's a property my family owns in Connecticut. I want you to stay there until I figure out what to do about Patricia."

I was trying to keep up with his long-legged strides while processing what he had just said.

"I don't understand. Why are you trying to send me to Connecticut? This is not boarding school, and you're not my daddy."

Finally, he stopped, and his face was close to mine again. "I'm not trying to get you to do anything. I'm telling you what you're going to do. And this time I want you to fucking listen to me."

I jerked my head backward and then looked around the room. Shit, I had forgotten about the reporters, and they were watching us as if the two of us together were the biggest fish they had never even dreamed of catching.

"Mr. Spencer Christmas and Miss Forte, are the two of you in a relationship?" a reporter called.

Lights flashed and cameras clicked. Even people who'd appeared sickly before Spencer's name was spoken had their cellphones pointing at us. Flexing his jaw, Spencer grabbed my hand.

"Change of plans," he muttered as we rushed out of the automatic doors, a horde of reporters following us.

A black sedan with tinted windows rolled to a stop in front of us.

Spencer opened the back door. "Get in."

I wanted to resist simply because I didn't like his tone, but the reporters were still shouting questions, asking how long we'd been together and did our relationship complicate the link between Patricia Forte and Dillon Gross. As soon as I heard that, I wanted to escape the chaos, so I quickly ducked into the back seat. I had forgotten about that particular mound of shit my mom was wading through. Spencer made sure I was completely in the car before slamming the door. He trotted around back of the vehicle and got in beside me.

"To the airport," Spencer told the driver.

I turned to look out the back window as the car sped away from the curb. The reporters looked confused about what to do next. They hadn't been prepared for Spencer and me to walk through the lobby together. It was too late to scamper to their vehicles and try to keep up with us, so one by one, they reentered the hospital.

When I faced forward, Spencer was glaring at me and I skipped a breath, feeling the full force of his ire.

I WAS TIRED AND MY HEAD FELT AS IF IT WERE lodged within a slowly closing vice.

"I'm not going to Connecticut," I said now that, other than the driver, Spencer and I were alone.

He scratched his temple as he sighed sharply. "Do you think this is a fucking game, Jada?" he grumbled, jerking his hand in a slicing motion.

Frankly, I was tired of bitter and mean Spencer. "No!" I shouted. "Why in the hell do you think I fought for the papers? It's not a fucking game. I know! My mother's a monster."

He paused, allowing his condemning eyes to soften just a smidgen. "Where did you find those papers anyway?"

I leaned away from him, shaking my head

adamantly. "Oh, no... Me first. Who the hell is Irina Petrov?"

"That's nothing for you to concern yourself with."

I grunted thoughtfully. "Let's see... You show up at the hospital and save me from whatever my mother had planned for me, which I am thankful for. And in my heightened state of emotional confusion, you order me to follow you. I left my rental car behind, which I am responsible for, you know. You want to tuck me away in some fortress in Connecticut. And now, you're telling me Irina Petrov isn't my concern?" I had said a mouthful without pause, and now I was dizzy from overexcitement and the lack of oxygen. However, I mustered up enough energy to shout, "Fuck you, Spencer!" I tapped the back of the driver's seat. "Let me out."

The driver turned just enough to glance at Spencer through his rearview mirror without slowing his speed.

I was prepared to shout it again. If the driver chose to keep going, I was in such a state that I was prepared to open the door and roll out onto the pavement.

"Enough, Jada!" Spencer roared.

"Enough with the controlling act. I don't like it, and you know it."

Spencer huffed as he studied me contemplatively. Then he shifted abruptly to scratch the back of his neck. "Irina is someone who was associated with my father."

I set my jaw. "I got that part. What else?"

He narrowed an eye. "I don't know what else."

I faintly believed him. At least some of the tightness fell out of my body. "Okay, but why would my mother say Irina's name as a way to threaten you?"

He shook his head. "I have no idea, Jada. Irina's dead. Her remains were found in the cement. That's why…" He leaned away from me, pressing his scrumptious lips into a flat line. I've seen that expression from him way too often to not know what it meant.

"You still think you can't trust me, Spencer?" I threw my hands up in defeat. "Holy shit, I just tussled with my mom's bodyguard. Isn't that enough to make you believe I'm no longer on her side?"

"And don't ever do anything like that again. He could've hurt you very badly, Jada. A man who's functioning on pure adrenaline could kill a woman your size."

Now that I was winding down from the excitement, my body was feeling exactly what he said. My shoulder and hip, which had hit the floor, had a dull ache. However, there was no way I was going to mention that to Spencer.

I sighed, hanging my head. "I wasn't thinking clearly."

I waited to hear him say he told me so, but when he didn't, I looked up at his face. I had no idea why each time I saw him this close, it felt as if I'd been looking into his eyes ever since the day I was born. My heart pounded like crazy. My lips desired contact. Spencer swallowed. I could feel and see the same lust that flowed from me coming from him. But he leaned away from me, coughed, and gazed ahead.

"Jada, I would still like for you to stay at my family estate in Connecticut. You will be safe there until all of this clears up." He was being very careful about his tone and was choosing his words wisely. "The estate is not like the ranch. The pool is easier to access, you can go horseback riding, paddling... There's a movie theater..."

I closed my eyes and breathed in deeply through my nostrils. "Spencer?" I said with a sigh. "I haven't watched a movie since college."

He was silent.

I kept my eyes closed. "I want to stay with you. Can I please stay with you?"

I opened my eyes, and he was watching me once again with fire and desire.

We stared at each other, and after a long moment, he nodded.

"Thank you," I whispered breathily.

He stared at my lips as if he were dazed. I waited impatiently for Spencer to gather me in his arms and lower me to the seat so we could make out feverishly. Instead, he scooted closer to the door, clearly putting more distance between us, then turned to look out the window.

I sat trapped in indecision, not knowing what to say or do. It was clear he was angry about having to save me from my mother's goon and then the shit she had said about him. Maybe he was having a hard time separating me from Senator Forte. However, I didn't like the silence between us. I couldn't trust it.

"So, what about my rental car?" I asked.

"Don't worry about it. I'll handle it."

My expression fluttered from tight to looser. "Then what about us?"

Finally, he looked at me again. "I don't know about us, Jada."

"Really?" I felt and sounded so sad.

His eyebrows ruffled even more. "Let's not talk about this right now."

I didn't want to let it go. I wanted him to say he still loved me and couldn't live without me. I wanted him to explain at which point he had questioned his feelings for me.

"You don't love me anymore because of my mom?" My voice was shaky.

Spencer refused to look at me when he said, "I never said I didn't love you."

My gaze expanded as I watched him longingly, willing him to face me, take me, and reassure me of what he felt about me with more vigor than he'd just done. But Spencer continued staring out the window, and in a snap decision, I chose not to push and instead go with the flow. Plus, as long as I was with him, he would break. At some point he would take me, make love to me, and tell me he couldn't live without me—not now, but soon. I was sure it would be very soon.

CHAPTER THREE

JADA FORTE

W e drove through the gated entrance for those with private flights. Before we boarded the aircraft, Spencer had me hand the keys for my rental car to the woman working behind the counter, who assured him she would have the vehicle returned to the rental company within the hour.

"Make sure all charges are put on my account," Spencer said with a brisk nod.

The woman displayed her obligatory smile. "Yes, Mr. Christmas."

Then I remembered something and gasped as I slapped my chest. "My luggage."

Spencer nodded calmly. "Have someone bring her luggage. I don't want to take off without it."

"Yes, Mr. Christmas," she said, her smile still indicating she was happy to serve him.

I caught a glimpse of our aircraft as we approached the ramp. It was the size of a large airplane. The one we took from Wyoming to Santa Barbara on Christmas Eve last year was only half the size. Spencer instructed me to board without him. He had some details to take care of first. As soon as I stepped into the cabin, I was unexpectedly awestricken by the scale of its luxuriousness. Four fluffy, off-white leather reclining chairs, two next to each other and facing their counterparts, with a long wooden block table sliced into four parts sat on one side of the aisle. A matching leather sofa sat on the other. The flooring was thick orange carpet with a Persian rug pattern throughout. The flight attendant, a bouncy young woman about my age, informed me the bathroom had robes and slippers as well as all the accoutrements of home. She then asked if I would like a beverage, and I ordered sparkling water with lemon.

I buckled into a seat near the window. Spencer was still MIA. The longer I sat, the more I believed he had tricked me and had actually put me on a flight to Connecticut. My eyes shifted nervously from left to right. *How could I have been so easily duped?*

I should've remained by his side. I pulled my phone out of my purse and turned it on, but before I could call Spencer, my phone rang. I read the name on the screen and immediately tapped Answer.

I scooted to the edge of my seat. "Dad?"

"Your brother's been released, and I received a call from the chief of police expressing his humble apologies," he said. "How did you do it?"

That was good to hear, and I was even more relieved when Spencer walked on board. When the flight attendant asked what he'd be drinking, he said he'd have what I ordered.

"Jada?" my dad asked.

"Sorry, Dad," I said loud enough for Spencer to hear me.

He locked eyes with me and situated himself in the aisle seat across from me. I was flabbergasted by the distance he'd chosen to put between us.

"What did you say to your mother that made her put a stop to her shenanigans?"

"Um…" I said, distracted by the flight attendant setting a drink in front of Spencer.

"Thank you, April," he said and then hit a button on the arm of his chair. His portion of the wooden table rose, stopping at where he could comfortably reach his drink.

"Darling, where are you?" my father asked, clearly noticing how distracted I was.

"I'm on an airplane. I can't take long. All I can say is that I'm glad everything worked out."

"Well, whatever you did, I'm thankful. I'm not able to get through to her anymore." My father sounded as if he wanted to engage in a longer conversation of all the ways my mom had changed for the worse.

I kept my glistening eyes pasted on Spencer as I cleared my throat. "Yes, she was quite difficult to reason with." I adjusted abruptly in my seat. "Dad, I have to go."

"Where are you flying to at this hour anyway, back to New York?"

I didn't want to lie to him. "Can I call you later?"

He paused. Normally, I would just hang up to make sure to not tell him a lie, but this time I wanted to handle avoidance differently. "Dad, I'm fine. I promise you, I'm safe. I love you but I'm going to hang up now. Good night?"

Spencer looked up from his phone to study me curiously. I turned away from his examination.

"Good night," my dad said before I could push the End button.

I tipped my head to the side. "Really? That was easy."

My dad chuckled. "If you don't want to tell me where you're going, and you say you're safe, then I believe you." He paused for a beat. "Are you with Spencer Christmas?"

Even though Spencer was typing on his phone, I could tell he was hanging on to my every word.

"Yes," I said.

"I see... Then the two of you are still a couple after what happened on Christmas Eve?" he asked.

Suddenly, the desire to ditch my father left me. "Does that upset you?"

"No. Your mom instigated the whole fucking scene. And I'm relieved it's out there, although I wish I would've told you myself. When it comes to her, I'm weak."

"You're not weak, Dad," I said instinctively even though I didn't believe it, at least when it came to my mother.

Silence fell between us. Thank goodness the pilot announced we were heading to the runway. My dad said he would like for Stefan and me to meet one day. I said that'd be fine, we said our final goodbyes, and I put my phone in airplane mode.

I felt myself watching Spencer longingly,

wanting to ask if this was how we were going to spend our flight—apart from each other and in our own mental universes. Then April walked into the cabin to announce that for dinner we would be having surf and turf over chilled fresh mint pesto with linguine, oysters on a bed of asparagus, and a fresh greens salad with lemon honey vinaigrette.

My stomach growled just thinking about food. The more I came down from the excitement of what happened less than an hour ago, the hungrier I became. Not only that but my skin felt clammy, and the scent of my stress sweat was nearly unbearable.

"Excuse me," I said to April after she finished telling us which wines were paired with dinner.

She raised her eyebrows, showing me an open expression. "Yes, Miss Forte?"

I lifted my arms to get a distant whiff of my armpits. "You said there was a shower?"

Finally, Spencer looked at me.

"Yes, it's in the rear of the aircraft," she said.

Spencer swiftly readjusted in his seat. "That'll be all for now, April."

The flight attendant nodded at Spencer and disappeared into a cabin across from the entrance. My heart was on edge and so was my curiosity.

I narrowed an eye thoughtfully, wondering why he'd dismissed our flight attendant so suddenly after I inquired about a shower.

"She did tell me there were towels and a robe. Am I not—"

"I know what's in the bathroom," he said, cutting me off.

I shook my head like a rattle, then threw up my hands. "What the hell, Spencer?"

I watched him in heightened anticipation as his table lowered. Then, he unclicked his seatbelt and rose to his feet. I felt choked as he walked toward me and unlatched my seatbelt. His nearness made me want to pass out. Then he took me by my hands, lifted me to my feet, and guided me into the aisle.

Finally, I was in his embrace again, and my head was woozy with gratification.

"Jada," he whispered, his warm breath against my neck. Then I felt his tongue and teeth grazing my skin in the same spot. A tingle raced up my thighs, gripping my pussy.

"Yes," I said with a sigh, eyelids fluttering, caught in a state of euphoria.

"I need a moment, baby." He made out with my neck some more, rousing sensations that fizzled from my nipples downward. "You taste so damn good," he whispered and then drove his tongue deep into my mouth.

My head felt silky as my tongue engaged with his. Then he gently kissed me on my lips.

"A lot has happened tonight," he whispered. "I need space to process." Eyes closed; he pasted his forehead against mine.

"I'm here, Spencer," I whispered.

He didn't say anything.

"Process with me. We should work this out together, don't you think?"

Spencer's forehead abandoned mine, and he gazed into my eyes as if he'd awakened from a trance.

The captain announced we were next in line for takeoff. Then he told us our flight would be seven hours, and other than catching a little weather along the way, we should soar smoothly all the way to Toronto.

When Spencer went back toward his seat, I sighed solemnly and then turned to secure myself in mine. However, he was heading toward me again, carrying his drink. I felt my face beaming at him as he sat beside me.

He clicked my seatbelt and then his. Once we

were compliant with the captain's orders, Spencer cupped the side of my face and we were kissing again. Around in circles my head ran as our tongues pressed, rubbed, and brushed each other. I moaned because I couldn't get close enough to him. Even as the aircraft darted down the runway, our mouths didn't let go of each other.

When we were in the air, April's voice came through the speaker letting us know dinner would be served shortly. Spencer got up and sat across from me to eat dinner. I couldn't figure out why he needed to shift his position, but I was happy he didn't take the aisle seat opposite of me.

CHAPTER FOUR

JADA FORTE

I t didn't take long for April to roll out our first and second courses. The food was so delicious that the flavors came alive in my mouth. Spencer stopped engaging with his cellphone long enough to brag about the chef who had prepared our meal. His name was Chef Bartholomew Winthrop, a man who had been trained at some of the best culinary academies in the world. He also won a Jon Ripley Award, for outstanding private chefs, six times in his career and had been working for the Christmas family for the past fifteen years. However, with the help of Spencer's sister-in-law Holly, Chef Bart was slated to open his own restaurant in Napa Valley next year.

I thought it was impressive and loved hearing Spencer tell me all about the man named Chef Bart, who he clearly had great admiration for, especially since it was the most he'd said to me on any subject since we had left the hospital.

"Wow, Napa Valley?" I asked to keep him talking.

"Yes, my family has owned a vineyard there ever since the end of Prohibition." There was a distance in his tone that drove me crazy. I wanted like hell to bridge our gap.

I was about to ask what sort of wine they produced when April was back with our third course. The oysters and asparagus were delectably plated. My first bite nearly melted in my mouth. "Mmm…" I said while chewing.

Spencer watched me as if he was conflicted.

"What?" I asked.

He shook his head and went back to whatever he was doing on his cellphone. He apparently received Internet service I wasn't privy to. It didn't matter because now that my tummy was nearly satiated, all I wanted was to shower and then return to my seat and sleep.

After dessert was served, Spencer finally looked up at me after I made another noise.

I threw my hands up. "Sorry. The food is out of this world."

His eyes smoldered as he inhaled deeply through his nostrils. "You're not bothering me, Jada. Not at all." He cleared his throat and then swallowed. "By the way, your friend is happy you're okay."

I frowned for a moment. "Oh, Hope."

"Yes." He went back to focusing on whatever had him so occupied with his phone.

"Sexting?" I finally asked and then put a spoonful of the richest, most flavorful vanilla custard I'd ever tasted into my mouth. I rolled my eyes a little, enjoying that bite even more than the last.

Spencer smirked. "You know you can have seconds and thirds if you like."

I narrowed an eye suspiciously. "You never answered my question. Who are you sexting?"

"I'm sexting no one."

I pressed my lips, nodding. No one knew how to put an end to my digging faster than Spencer could.

I made another spoonful of custard ready to go into my mouth. "I guess I'll take a shower next, try to wash off some of the energy and stench of what happened earlier. Or would you rather I not shower?" I worked like hell to not close my eyes to savor the flavors.

He looked up from his phone. "You have free reign of my airplane. You can do what you want."

I raised an eyebrow inquisitively. "You own this aircraft?"

"Yes."

It was is if his gaze was undressing me one garment at a time. At least he was still sexually attracted to me.

"It's about my mom, isn't it?" I asked.

"What do you mean?" His tone was gentler.

I put down my spoon. I didn't want to say what I was thinking because it felt as if I had made a little headway with him as far as softening up toward me —just a little. But I wanted to put everything that could be causing the distance between us out on the table, so I said it anyway. "What she said about you as a teenager."

His eyebrows ruffled and then evened out. "That didn't bother me."

I forced myself to remain the picture of repose, even though his conversation-bursting answers made me want to scream. "I feel as if you're purposely putting distance between us."

Spencer sighed wearily and then scratched the

back of his neck. "I don't know what else to say to you, Jada."

"I know you need to process, but…" I sat up straight, struck by a series of memories flashing through my head. I saw my mom, instructing Hugh to take the documents from me and then after that imprison me. Had she thought I would just give them up without a fight? Then Hugh had tried to carry out his orders and I'd hit the ground. Spencer had saved me.

"I'm going to shower," I muttered and stood abruptly. If he wanted to take some emotional distance to figure out what he felt about me, then I would give it to him. After what he'd done for me in that hospital room, it was the least I could do for Spencer. "Oh and thank you for coming to my rescue. I truly appreciate it."

I didn't wait for his response. I walked so fast out of the cabin that my head spun.

THE FIRST DOOR I OPENED REVEALED A LUSH bedroom. The second door was the bathroom I was looking for, which could've been featured in one of those old episodes of *Pimp My Ride* or house or private jet airplane. In the center of the space stood a shower that resembled a glass chamber. An ultramodern, double-sink vanity was against the wall, and it had two wooden shelves beneath it that held white towels of three sizes. Next to that was a rack where the robes were hanging, and beneath them were white slippers. In a hurry, I stripped bare. It was a relief to get those clothes off me. I folded my garments and set them on the sink. Then I turned on the shower and stepped into the warm water.

April had been right. All the essentials were at my fingertips, like a delicious-smelling soap and shampoo. I lathered my body and my hair. The plane jolted—turbulence—but I remained steady on my feet and continued basking in the warmth. I didn't expect Spencer to join me. I didn't even want him to. I now wanted the same distance he sought.

There was a reality I was coming to grips with. Other than the money in my bank account, which I hadn't had to touch much ever since working for Jimmy's campaign, I had nothing. I didn't have my apartment in Manhattan anymore. I didn't have a job. And the thought of going through the process of applying and interviewing filled me with dread. Then I remembered my mother had access to my bank account. That would be the first thing I would change once I got back to life as usual, and it baffled me why I hadn't done it yet. Had I been hanging onto my mother while convincing myself I had been running away from her? Had I made her my convenient safety net?

As the warm water slid through my hair and gripped my scalp, I thought about how my mom used to sit with me for hours until I became an expert at solving multiple trigonometry computations. I had always admired that about my mom. Many of my friends had parents who couldn't do that kind of math, but my mom could. She was intelligent—a genius actually. Also, whenever I had boyfriend problems, I could talk to her, knowing she wouldn't judge me. Mom would listen attentively, and when I'd arrive at the end of my rant, she would ask, "Do you feel better now that you've gotten that off your chest?" Of course I would say I felt better. Then she would follow up with a gracious smile and another version of her words of wisdom, which always could be summarized as: "I had my whole life ahead of me and so did the boy who had me all in a huff. In ten years, neither of us would recognize who we were at that moment in time."

"At this stage in your life, sweetheart, your

friends and boyfriends are part of your learning process, so there's no need to be so fatalistic about them." Her smile would grow wider as she took me by the shoulders. "So thank them for giving you the opportunity to perfect yourself."

That was my mom in a nutshell, which was why I could hardly believe she knew about Randolph Christmas, and instead of launching an investigation and turning him into the authorities, she had extorted him for campaign money. Also, taking donations from foreign governments? I could hardly believe she was the same woman who used to teach me math and give me relationship advice that would last a lifetime.

The shower water washed my tears down the drain. I wondered if it was okay to still be so very much in love with the versions of my mother I admired. Would Spencer understand that? He was lucky his father was dead and buried. I was sure that made it easier for him to move forward. He also had siblings he'd grown up with. I was alone. He wasn't.

When I turned the water off, I had come to a decision. As I stepped out of the shower, the door opened, and my heart stopped. It was Spencer.

CHAPTER FIVE

JADA FORTE

I could feel the lust coming off him like smoke snaking up from the ashes. The water dripping from my skin made a puddle around my feet.

"Don't move," he whispered and then coughed to clear his throat.

His gaze slid up and down my nakedness, raising his eyebrows a hair higher when glancing at his favorite parts. Finally, Spencer walked over to take a towel off a wooden shelf. I could hardly breathe and didn't want to speak as he brushed the rich, soft fibers against my tits and down my belly. He released a random breath, eyes glaring at my nipples before stepping around to my rear to slide the towel from my upper back down to my ass. He dried my thighs, legs, and finally the top of my feet. He looked up at me while he squatted. Trapped in suspense, my mouth fell open. Spencer stood and slid the towel down my hair. He wiped any remnants of water off my shoulders and back and then dropped the towel on the floor.

"I'm all dry," I finally said, although my pussy was soaking wet.

Spencer narrowed an eye, as if warning me to remain silent, then took my hand and led me through a door that opened to the bedroom. He walked me to the foot of the king-sized bed and pressed my shoulders down, beckoning me to sit. As soon as my ass hit the firm mattress, Spencer dropped to his knees and positioned his shoulders under my thighs, and I sighed as my pussy made contact with his soft mouth.

First, Spencer indulged in my pussy lips, sucking them delicately and licking them. Our gazes remained locked as I watched him eat me out. There was a dare in his eyes. I could tell he wasn't satisfied with my calm disposition, and that's when his tongue rounded my clit. I let out a yelp and flung myself against the mattress as he continued stimulating my hard knot. I squirmed, trying to twist my pussy away from his mouth to win just a second of reprieve, but Spencer had a vice grip on my lower half. As usual, the idea that he was strong made me cream some more.

"Oh," I cried, over and over again.

He was completely in charge, especially as the exhilaration of a potent orgasm surged throughout my pussy. When I cried out, it was as if I had left my body and was on the verge of whiting out. I squirmed when he finally let go of me. His mouth wasn't on my clit anymore, but the pleasure was still with me.

I heard his pants unzip. One deep breath and I turned to watch him step out of his pants and pull down his underwear. My eyes expanded with desire as his thick cock sprang forward. Then his bare chest stole my attention. His physical fitness gave Michelangelo's *David* a run for his money. I spread my legs to receive my lover. Spencer slid up my body but stopped to sink one of my tits deep into his mouth, then his tongue rounded my nipple before he delicately raked his teeth against the tip. The pleasurable sensations drove me crazy. I moaned and sighed, pushing my tits against his mouth, and when the pleasure became too much, I attempted to draw away from his mouth.

After licking my nipple one last time, he did the

same to my other breast. For a second, I was able to open my eyes. Spencer's eyes were closed too. He rarely closed his eyes when experiencing my body. He seemed lost in his own pleasure and desire. I was satisfied, and I moaned his name to let him know.

Spencer whimpered as he quickly opened a drawer on the nightstand by the bed. He took out a condom and ripped it open. My pussy wept for him as he slid the rubber over his cock and then positioned himself between my thighs before slamming his cock deep inside me. I cried out, feeling his manhood surge toward my belly and hit bottom. I inhaled with his every deep thrust into my sex. It was all as it had been the night before I took off to Santa Barbara to see about my mother's health. His hard body against mine. His cock opening me wide. Electric sensations stirring inside me.

Spencer's mouth soon found mine, and we tongued each other as he drove his shaft in and out of me. I became lost in our activity. Momentarily I'd forgotten how we got here and where we were going. All that mattered was the here and now.

My body tensed when Spencer's thick cock slid against a familiar and sensitive spot. As usual, my quickening hadn't gone unnoticed. He stimulated the area more and more. The noises I made as my orgasm took form were new to me. I was overly excited. He wouldn't stop rousing that spot. My body was tight down to my toes, and for that his tongue dove deeper into my mouth. We both whimpered and then it happened for me, orgasmic sensations spreading through me like electrical currents. Then he called for the Almighty, and his body shivered and quaked like never before.

———

IT WAS AS I HAD THOUGHT. SPENCER WAS AS ravenous for me as I was for him. Even after we both came together, we made out like crazy, our tongues and lips unable to break loose. Just when I thought we would stop, I became hungrier for him, and my mouth chased his. The same happened with him. If our lips broke just for a second, Spencer's would greedily seek mine out again. He clamped me tight against him, and I tried to do the same. More kissing. More rubbing. More licking and biting. Then he was up, putting on another condom, and was inside me again. His thrusts were deep and indulgent, our gazes glued to each other. Our breaths crashed, first slowly, then as he increased pace, quickly. He grabbed the headboard and threw all his strength into plunging deep inside me before bellowing, "Oh!" as he quaked.

When Spencer rolled me over to lie on top of him, his deflating dick still inside me, I closed my eyes and he kissed my forehead.

"Sleep, baby," he said. "But I want to stay inside you."

I was all out of energy, and I may have said or grunted, "Okay," before drifting off.

"PLEASE PREPARE FOR LANDING," APRIL'S VOICE said, coming in through the speakers.

My eyes fluttered open. I had fallen asleep on top of Spencer, but now I was alone in the large bed. I would've questioned whether we actually made love if my pussy wasn't still throbbing from being penetrated by his thickness. And I was still wet.

I was about to get up and wash up and put my stinky clothes back on when Spencer entered from the bathroom. He had a towel wrapped around his lower half and was beaming.

"Don't worry about the warning, baby," he said

and pulled his towel loose. "It's going to take less than fifteen minutes to do you." Spencer was guiding me back onto the bed. My thighs were opened, and he slid his manhood, which was already fitted with a condom, indulgently into my wetness.

After he came, Spencer shuffled back into the bathroom and returned with a wet and warm face towel. He carefully wiped my pussy, sipping air as he kept his eyes on my mound.

"How did you like it?" he finally asked.

"Our sex?" I asked for clarification.

He smirked naughtily. "Yeah."

"I loved it."

Spencer dropped the towel on the floor and lay beside me. "I couldn't resist you," he said with a sigh.

I snorted. "I'm glad you stopped trying."

After a long pause, he said, "Me too."

Silence lingered. My body was like tiny tentacles still reaching for his stimulation. Ever since I gave Spencer my virginity, it was as if when we lay together, naked and alone, I couldn't stop craving him inside me.

"There's something I want to say to you," he finally whispered.

Instantly I became worried. "Okay." I sounded hesitant, hoping what we just had wasn't goodbye sex.

Spencer reached over and hit a button on the wall beside the white, high-gloss nightstand, its top outlined by blue lights.

"April?" he called.

"Yes, Mr. Christmas?"

"We'll prepare for landing in the bedroom."

She paused for a second and then said, "Yes, Mr. Christmas."

Now that that was over, Spencer pasted his focus back on me. Damn he was so good looking. I wondered how long I would have the opportunity to wake beside his sexy face.

"I don't want you internalizing what happened in that hospital room." He tilted his head and intensified his focus on me. "Okay?"

I nodded. "Thank you," I whispered past the tightness in my throat.

"I wondered how you mother could've found out about what my dad put me through as a kid. The only way she could've known was if you told her…"

I gasped sharply, shaking my head vigorously in my own defense. "I didn't."

His warm hand soothingly rubbed the inside of my thigh. "I know. I was messaging my brother, and he believes our father offered all those who were blackmailing him insurance before he died."

He went on to tell me how his father knew he would die soon long before the final heart attack and stroke had made him bed-ridden and comatose. At some point, word had got out that he was sick, and Spencer's older brother Jasper had noticed his father taking meetings with a lot of people. My mom was one of those people.

Since we were finally having the difficult conversation, it was time to ask the hard questions.

"Did you know about my mother and father before you hired me?"

"Yes," Spencer replied without hesitation. "When I saw your resume, I was shocked and intrigued." He scoffed. "I actually laughed. Not in a million fucking years did I ever believe Forte's daughter would answer my job announcement. But you did." He turned to gaze at me. "And here you are."

My breaths caught, and I wanted to kiss him, but he stared at the ceiling again.

"I've already told you this, but I knew you would be handling my most private and sensitive data, which was why I had my investigators perform a thorough background check on you."

I turned to lie on my side. "I remember you telling me that. What all did they find?"

"You'd been living away from your mother for the past six years. Also, you didn't know she'd secured you your job at Caldwell Jamison." He studied me, I guessed to see if I'd known that.

I shrugged. "I didn't know but I'm not surprised." It would've bothered me then if I had known, and I was 100 percent sure I would've quit my job.

Spencer grunted thoughtfully. "You were fired after Sam North sold the company to Genie Corp. Griffin Mortimer was a supporter of Todd Branson. Do you know who that is?"

"Of course," I said. "He opposes everything she brings to the floor. My mom actually campaigned against his reelection. She got close to ousting him, but he pulled some shit with the recount to keep his seat." I suddenly slapped a hand on my chest as I sat up. "Wait! Then she knew."

He frowned. "She knew what?"

"That I lost my job and was living off my savings."

"I'm sure she did," he replied.

I squeezed my eyes tight as my mind put the pieces together. I wanted to stop the action, but it was too late. My mom knew I was going through financial hardship, which meant she could've been the reason behind why no one would hire me. She knew just about everyone in the corporate industry. My entire life, every job, friend, boyfriend, and school considered my last name and who I was related to before deciding to engage with me. But she had no pull when it came to Spencer. It was the opposite. He was a threat to her.

"It never made sense to me why she disliked you so much. You're powerful." I threw up my hands. "I mean, look what you own. I would've thought she would've seen my association with you as an opportunity. But she came at you with an aggression that was nothing like I'd ever seen from her, and now I know why." I closed my eyes and sighed gravely. "You can destroy the one thing she's ever loved more than me or my dad, and that is her career."

Spencer and I stared into each other's eyes. I guessed he was assessing the fallout. If he took my mother down, would he lose me? I, on the other hand, was remembering Alice's offer.

We both started to speak at the same time.

Spencer nodded. "Ladies first."

I smiled warmly, appreciating the small things that endeared Spencer to me. "Why don't you run against Jimmy?"

He shook his head as if it were the most ridiculous suggestion he'd ever heard. Then he looked at me with a lopsided smile. "Are you fucking serious?"

I flexed my eyebrows twice, feeling emboldened. "As a heart attack." I readjusted to sit on my legs. "Let's do it, Spencer."

He shook his head continuously while studying me curiously. "But you would do that, operate against your mother politically?"

I set my jaw, getting a high from what I was about to say. "Absolutely."

Spencer's eyes narrowed and smoldered as he reached out to pull me under him. The captain announced we would be landing in five minutes.

Spencer looked over his shoulder at the door. He contemplated. My pussy throbbed, desiring to swallow his manhood.

"Ah, fuck it," he said.

I gasped as his thickness raced into me.

THE AIRCRAFT HAD LANDED, AND THE CAPTAIN

announced we were ready to disembark when I came, and Spencer quaked with orgasm shortly thereafter. We weren't done yet though. Knowing we had to disembark sooner rather than later, we rolled around on the bed, making out, never being able to get enough of each other.

"Shit," he said, breathing heavily. "We have to hit the road." Spencer sat up on the side of the bed, rubbing his temples.

He turned to gaze at my nakedness. The desire in his eyes made me writhe with want. We both admitted we could lie in bed and make love to each other for eons, but we were pressed for time. Spencer shot to his feet and dressed himself. He left me to take a quick shower and to tame my wild hair as he went to confirm the logistics connected to our arrival to our next destination.

After showering and blow-drying my hair, I put on my jeans, two sweaters, and two pairs of socks with my ankle boots. I knew it would be cold as an icebox in Toronto, and only while dressing myself did I realize I had nothing in my suitcase to keep me from freezing my ass off. However, I was the one who had insisted on flying to Toronto with Spencer. Therefore, it was my responsibility to suck it up and carry on.

When I walked into the front cabin, April was waiting by the door with a huge smile. I thanked her for serving us during the flight. She said I was welcome and handed me my stylish but flimsy leather jacket and my purse. On my first step out of the cabin and down the ramp, I recoiled as the light of the muted daylight, made bright by snow layering the uncemented terrain, jabbed me in the eyes. A black town car was parked at the bottom of the ramp. My legs were wobbly, probably still from all the dopamine released from my brain to my body while making love and being intimate with Spencer. With each step down, I realized it was just as I'd thought, cold as hell outside and my stylish jacket and two sweaters weren't doing the trick well enough.

The back door of the car opened, and Spencer stepped out and held it open for me. His expression was back to being all business. I preferred the more amiable Spencer Christmas. It was too chilly to test if a flirty smile or a sexier walk could get him to lighten up a bit. I moved swiftly, and once my butt hit the seat, I held myself and shivered as the warmth from the air vents began to unfreeze my blood.

Not until Spencer slid in beside me did I realize he wore a long, thick, and appropriate winter coat.

He studied me—his eyes pinched a little as he rubbed the side of his nose. "We'll have to get you a coat at some point. I don't want you getting sick."

I shuddered as tempered air continued to defrost me. "It's so cold I can use some of the heat a body generates when a person has a fever. Except, I don't want to be the one with the fever. I want to be next to the person with the fever." I shook my head. What the hell was I saying? The cold must've rattled my brain.

It happened so fast that if I blinked, I would've missed it. Spencer's eyebrows fluttered slightly, as if his desire had been stirred by the idea of me being bedridden, and his dick was inside me, being heated by my hot, feverish body.

Spencer cleared his throat. "Tony, let's go."

The car rolled carefully to the gate where the guard waved us through instead of stopping us.

"Are you going to tell me where we're going now?" I asked while gazing out the window, taking in the clean, crisp allure of one of my favorite cities.

"We're paying Irina's sister, Nadia, a visit," he said, glaring ahead with laser focus.

My eyebrows furrowed. "Does she know you're coming?"

Spencer set his intense eyes on me. "No."

I skipped a breath. The way he looked at me almost made me want to zip it up and not ask another question. However, he knew very well that I wasn't the sort of person who could be intimidated into silence.

"Are we going to her house?" I asked.

"No." He squeezed his lips together. "She owns a café downtown."

I jerked my head backward a little. "Oh, which one?" I loved Toronto and had come often with a group of girlfriends to frequent the many bars and cafés and engage in the young singles night scene. I'd never scored any prospects after our adventures. Hope had said it was because I wasn't as motivated as the others, and neither was she. I never truly understood what the hell she'd meant by that until this very moment while riding in the car with Spencer Christmas. I had never been so motivated to give my body and soul to a man until him.

He mumbled the name of the establishment, and I was sure it was killing him to be so frank with me.

"I'm sorry, what did you say?" I asked.

Spencer cleared his throat as he abruptly adjusted himself in his seat. "Brown's Café."

My lips eased their way into a big smile. "See, that didn't hurt, did it?"

The corners of his mouth played with a smirk. "You look beautiful by the way."

I felt my cheeks warm. "Thank you."

Our gazes remained stuck on each other for a moment.

"Listen, how about you wait in the car while I go inside?" His voice was silky.

I leaned toward him, my expression full of amazement. "Wow, really, Spencer? Were you trying to butter me up with that beautiful comment?"

"What?" He cocked his head jerkily. "No. I've been trying to keep you safe, Jada, but you've been making it difficult."

I threw up my hands. "It's a café in Toronto. How dangerous could it be?"

Spencer's mouth twitched as he gazed off thoughtfully. By now I knew my best recourse of action was to wait until his deliberating ended.

"Jada," he finally said. "You being with me in this car is dangerous enough."

I shook my head like a rattle. "Then why doesn't it feel dangerous?"

He frowned as if my question had thrown him for a loop. In fact, I was hoping it would. Spencer was a deep thinker, which was another thing I loved about him. I had never been turned on by exquisitely handsome men who where intellectually challenged.

"Jada, I don't know much about this woman or who she's connected with. She is the sister of a wanted woman, and you don't get through that many years of not being questioned or handled without making deals with devils."

I grunted thoughtfully. I knew all about deals with devils and how soft and cuddly those deals appeared on the outside.

"I understand," I said, mildly acquiescing. "However, I think I can be of some help, Spencer. I have good instincts." He was about to speak, but I raised a hand to stop him. "I know you have good instincts too, but two pairs of eyes are better than one. How about I go in after you just to provide you another take on the scene?"

He twisted his head, narrowing an eye. "I don't know, Jada."

"Come on, Spencer." My pleading sounded like

severe whining, which certainly would've displeased my mother if she'd heard it. "Please. I didn't come all this way to sit in the car. I find it…" I frowned to think of the appropriate word, and the patience he exhibited while waiting took his sexual appeal up another notch. "Belittling."

He jerked his head as if he was taken aback. "You know I would never belittle you." The look in his eyes demanded that I respond.

"I know you wouldn't. And I know you're not trying to. But to keep the little lady in the car away from the danger…" I drew air quotes when I said danger. "That's belittling."

He set his jaw. "I don't agree. I'm protecting you from a man who's morally corrupt and has no regard for human life."

I turned my head slightly and studied him with raised eyebrows. "You said a lot there, buddy, without saying a lot."

Spencer sighed forcefully. "Shit, Jada, this fucking conversation is giving me a headache. Just stay in the car."

I folded my arms. "What if I don't?"

He pointed at his driver. "Then John will lock you inside."

My mouth fell open, and I gasped exaggeratedly. Without warning, Spencer's lips melted against mine. His tongue plunged deeply into my mouth. My chest rose toward his, my head did a few twirls, and the longer I tasted and devoured him, the more I started seeing things his way, which was why I ripped my lips away from his.

"Not fair," I snapped, trying to catch my breaths. I still felt intoxicated.

"Stay in the car. Check your email and messages. You know Hope's been looking for you."

I perked up. "I know. You told me that already." However, calling her sooner rather than later did appeal to me. We had a lot to talk about, especially since our last conversation ended with me hanging up on her. That was rude and I owed her an apology.

After a long moment, I sighed. "Spencer, I grew up in the shadow of Patricia Forte and have relationships with people like Alice Templeton, Marty Ashford, Dale Needle, and my father actually, who's also pretty shrewd underneath his nice guy exterior. So whoever this evil man I should be afraid of is, I'm pretty sure he's not as powerful and dangerous when crossed as any of those people I've mentioned."

"How long have you known your mother was corrupt?" he asked.

My mouth fell open. I hadn't expected him to ask that question. I scratched my eyebrow trying to get over the initial jolt of emotions racing through me. I felt his question was meant to prove my instincts weren't that great, but it wasn't how Spencer operated. If he asked me a question, then it was grounded in rationality and not insult.

I took in a deep breath through my nostrils and held it. I let the air saturate me through and through. It was time to be truthful not only with him but, more importantly, with myself.

"Frankly, Spencer, perhaps all my life." My voice cracked and tears welled in my eyes. I never wanted to say that out loud. But after what happened in the hospital, I was done deluding myself so I could respect my mother. I loved her though, and always would, but ignoring the fact that she threw her support behind guys like Jimmy Lovell, so he could be her political pawn, was on me, not her. It hadn't been the first time I'd seen her operate that way. I'd watched her stack Congress with allies for years. I never labeled her actions as manipulation and game play even though it was how I judged them. I had convinced myself that was how it went in politics. When in reality, it didn't have to.

Spencer sat very still and then shifted abruptly. "Ever heard of Arthur Valentine?"

The name almost choked me. I swallowed, unable to speak, and nodded.

We were stopped at a traffic light, and I faintly noticed cars slipping past us and pedestrians marching up the sidewalks, hovering to stay warm as they passed tall buildings.

"How?" he asked, scowling.

I felt my expression sour, just like my stomach. "I met him briefly."

Spencer scooted to the edge of his seat and craned his neck to study me intensely. "What did he do to you?" I heard controlled rage in his voice.

I started from the beginning. After graduating from college, I arrived in New York to start a new life away from my mother's control. But my last name, and the fact that Mom made sure everyone knew I was her daughter, had always followed me wherever I went. One night, Hope and I attended an invitation-only art gallery at the MoMA. The artist was Claude Jean Bernard. I had always believed the only reason I was sent that invitation and many others was because my mom had prompted them to do it. Normally, I would throw away the invites or give the really good tickets to a friend. But Claude Jean Bernard was arguably the best artist of the twenty-first century, and I wasn't going to miss an opportunity to shake his hand.

When Hope and I had arrived at the museum, we expected the place to be packed, but it wasn't. The carefully curated guests consisted of A-list actors and Grammy Award-winning musicians. Alice Templeton and others like her were there. At some point, after shaking hands and greeting old acquaintances of my mother's, I went to the ladies' room. When I stepped out of the stall, an old guy was washing his hands at the sink. When I apologized for going into the men's restroom by accident, he assured me I was in the right place.

"The next thing I knew, he had his hand around my throat and was pushing me up against the wall, nearly knocking the daylights out of me. He said he could fuck me and kill me right now and no one would care."

Spencer's face had turned beet red. If Valentine was in this car right now, I was positive Spencer would've ripped him to shreds.

I closed my eyes. I had buried that memory so far down inside me, it didn't even feel real anymore

—but it had been real. It had actually fucking happened.

"He told me to tell my mother that Arthur Valentine said stop. He said: 'And don't forget to tell her about this little incident between us.' I never felt so hopeful my whole life." My voice cracked. "Simply because if he was telling me to give my mother a message, it meant he wasn't going to kill me."

After a long moment, Spencer sat back in his seat and glared straight ahead. His lips were clamped, and he didn't move a muscle. I didn't know what to say, and I found myself wishing I would've kept the whole incident to myself. I had effectively made it no longer a part of my history. When I told my mother what had happened, she was calm. All she'd said was: "We Fortes are strong. Remember that. You don't have to be afraid of that man. I'll handle him. You will never see him again, ever." Her claim had been stalwart and true.

The driver announced we had arrived. I hadn't noticed our car had stopped along the curb. Finally, Spencer looked at me again.

"He put his hands on you," he said.

My lips parted. I wanted to answer but I was

pretty sure it wasn't a question, more like a statement.

He made sure to garner good eye contact with me. "I'm going in. Give me five minutes. If I'm not back, then you come in. We'll follow your suggestion. You'll sit at another table and watch." He nodded curtly, and I understood it was his way of asking if I was okay with his plan.

"Yes," I said. "Five minutes and then I come in."

He leaned forward to retrieve his wallet out of his back pocket. "Take this." He handed me three hundred dollars in Canadian currency.

I put up a hand, refusing to take it. "I can pay."

He pushed the cash toward me, insisting I take it. "You can't use your credit cards. Use this."

He made a lot of sense, and it was time to put my pride aside, so we went ahead with the plan. Spencer kissed me one last time before he opened the door and flowed out of the car. I watched his magnificence walk up the sidewalk. He garnered the attention of everyone he passed. He was that good looking. After a sigh to calm my nerves, I looked at my watch. Five minutes and I would go inside, just as we planned.

CHAPTER SIX

SPENCER CHRISTMAS

The bitter cold cut through my coat like a razor blade, and I was worried about Jada taking the same short walk in her thin jacket. Whenever I looked at her beautiful face and shapely feminine figure, all I wanted to do was keep her safe, secure, and tucked away somewhere inside me. I could've killed Patricia's henchman for putting his hands on her. It had taken every inch of self-control to keep him alive. And now Valentine? I added putting his filthy hands on the woman I loved to the long list of infractions he had to pay for.

I was too angry to be nervous, and I had to get that under control. I needed to have some uneasiness. I had my doubts about this sister of Irina's. I'd been in constant contact with Nestor, my private investigator. It seemed as if developments were updating at the speed of light. They had finally excavated all the bones out of the walls. Not all were complete skeletons. I'd told Nestor I wasn't shocked by that. It was in my father's style to be so concentrated, constantly trying to outsmart anyone who could catch him. It was why I had a team drag the grounds as well. No remains had turned up in the wilderness, but with all the animals constantly moving through the property, a predator could've dragged them off. The thought sent a chill down my spine as I stood at the counter, waiting my turn to speak to the blonde behind the register.

The newest development that really had me reeling was Nestor confirming that all they had found of Irina was the lower part of one of her legs. We'd both agreed that until we had Irina's complete skeletal remains, we had to operate as if she could still be alive. That had changed every-thing, which was why I had been so worried about Jada being with me. Anything could happen. Nestor had already confirmed no one other than his agents was keeping watch on the café from the outside, but he'd had no time to do an inside sweep, which meant I still had to be extra careful about who saw me with Nadia.

The woman working at the register was too young to possibly be Nadia, who I was told was in her late forties. Granted, I'd met many forty-year-old women who could pass for twenty-five, but I was sure the blonde was only in her twenties, especially by the way she watched me in a way that begged me to not only see her but appreciate her. They were the sort of daddy issues I used to take advantage of. Jada didn't have that problem though, and I often wondered how it had missed her.

"Hi, sir," the girl said, still beaming at me. "You can take a seat, and I'll be over to take your order."

I leaned closer to her and made sure I kept my voice low when I said, "I'm here to see Sarah Caldwell."

Nestor had confirmed Nadia's time of arrival, so I knew she was around somewhere.

The girl raised her eyebrows, continuing to grin, as her skin turned red. I was waiting for her to ask who I was. Nestor had advised me to tell her my name was Heinrich Deter. It was the alias he had used when he won their grandmother's trust well enough to get her to tell him how to find Nadia and the name she went by.

"Sure, have a seat and I'll go get her," the girl said without asking me to identify myself. That was a good sign. It meant Nadia didn't live with a lot of paranoia.

"Thank you," I said, positive she'd taken me as a suitor of Nadia's.

I didn't watch her traipse off through the door behind the counter, but I knew she went through it. I grabbed my seat, making sure it allowed me to keep my eyes on the door.

I loosened my shoulders, trying not to appear so stiff. I took a breath and looked around. Many of the seats were taken. Guys were working on their computers. Groups of people were locked in conversation. Women were watching me curiously. Then bells rang as the door opened, and in walked Jada.

Right away, I twisted my wrist to check my watch. It had been five minutes. I still thought her being here was a bad idea, but she had just as much of a claim to grab Valentine by the balls as I had. We locked eyes for a second, then she sat at one of the few empty tables on the opposite side of the room. As soon as she sat, the two guys at the table next to hers said something to her. One of the dudes made as if he were taking off his coat. She chuckled graciously. That fucker was offering it to her. I put my eyes on him, hoping he would look at me and feel the burn. She was not available, so back the hell off.

"Excuse me, sir," the girl from behind the register asked.

I ripped my attention away from what was happening on Jada's side of the room and forced myself to look at the girl.

"Sorry, I didn't get your…" She cocked her head, shaking a finger at me. "Wait, I know who you are. You're that rich American who found the bones."

I rubbed my forehead, wanting like hell to get up and rush into the back of the kitchen and force Nadia to face me. I had to think faster than I was, so I sat up straight.

"I'm not American, and I don't know anything about bones."

Her eyes narrowed a pinch, and she studied me some more. "Oh, then I apologize," she said weakly.

"Tell her Heinrich Deter is here to see her," I said.

When I gave her the fake name, she looked even more embarrassed. She told me Sarah would be with me soon and quickly walked away from the table. I could feel Jada looking at me, and when I turned toward her, I was right. I wanted badly to get up and go kiss her so that fucker would stop smiling at her.

I was sure she'd heard what the waitress asked because she started a full conversation with the guys to make them stop looking at me. Fuck, I hadn't known I was so fucking jealous. Later, when we're either back on the airplane or in a hotel room, for flirting with those two assholes in front of me, I was going to fuck her brains out. I pictured myself fucking her on her knees, my dick pounding her pussy. I could feel it, each thrust sending bolts of pleasure through my dick, sensations that had been elusive until I started making love to her.

"Hello," a woman said. Her voice had strokes of several different accents, and it was hard to pinpoint them all. Then she stepped into my line of sight, and I could no longer see Jada. I quickly rose to my feet.

"Hi," I said, assessing her.

She was attractive—oval face, high cheekbones, almond-shaped eyes, and pale skin. But her face was riddled by worry and frown lines.

Nadia remained unsmiling. "What do you want?"

I had expected her to be so blunt. "Could we talk?"

She folded her arms. "Once again, what do you want?"

"I want to talk to you about your sister and my father."

Her eyes fluttered open a little wider. Then she checked over both shoulders in a way that made me think she was figuring out the fastest path to run away from me.

"My father is dead. I have no loyalty to him," I assured her.

She sized me up. "You're Spencer Christmas, the man who discovered the girls' bodies?"

"Yes," I replied.

"Then why did you tell Misha you were someone else?"

I nodded, showing her that her question was fair. Then I shrugged. "My last name is Christmas. I didn't want to spook you."

"But your face is everywhere. You can't hide."

"I'm not looking to be anyone's hero. I did what I had to do. That's all. And I'm here because I want to know if your sister said anything about a man named Arthur Valentine."

"Follow me," she whispered. Nadia turned and

started walking. I followed her through the door behind the counter, down a dull hallway with concrete floors and dirty white walls, and into an office where everything was neatly placed.

"Sit," she said, her hand gesturing at a chair. Her Russian accent was more pronounced.

I sat.

She sat. "What do you want to know about my sister?"

"Is she alive?" I asked, trying to slip in an unexpected question and knock her off guard.

Nadia didn't flinch. "No."

"Did you know what sort of work she did for my father and Valentine?"

Her lip curled slightly. "Do you?"

"Yes, she ran a prostitute ring," I said, purposely being flagrant.

Anger flashed across her eyes as she scooted to the edge of her seat and stabbed the desktop with the tip of her finger. "My sister was a victim. She was not a criminal."

I got an emotional outburst out of her, which meant I had her on the ropes, and that was exactly where I wanted her. "The FBI doesn't think your sister wasn't a criminal," I said. "She was wanted for trafficking young girls with a guy named Klein."

Nadia jabbed the table again. "They are wrong. My sister was stolen from our home by the guy named Klein. What she did for him, she did to survive." She was visibly shaking.

"Do you have proof?" I asked.

After a moment, she sat back in her chair and narrowed her almond-shaped eyes at me. I figured she was contemplating whether to say more, so I thought it was best for me to help her along.

"If you want to clear your sister's name, then I'm the guy to tell whatever you know. I'm after one person, Arthur Valentine, not your sister."

She took a long and hard sigh before snatching a pencil out of a holder. I noticed all the erasers had been chewed, which explained why I felt an underbelly of nervous energy emanating from Nadia. Next, she opened the top drawer of her desk and moved around items in search of something.

"They move everything," she mumbled as she dropped a notebook on the desktop, opened it, and wrote down an address in Phoenix, Arizona, and two numerical codes. She ripped the sheet out of the notebook.

"What's that?" I asked.

"Go there. I have been paying for this for many years. I don't know what's inside, but my sister told me once that if I trust someone who wants to clear her name, then give them what I have given you." She handed me the paper.

I reached out to take it and then hesitated. "By the way, had she ever mentioned knowing who my mother was?" Shit, I felt like gasping for air. I couldn't believe I asked her that. It made me vulnerable in front of someone I only barely trusted.

Nadia shook her head, looking at me with a dull glint in her eyes. "She never mentioned it, no."

I nodded, accepting her answer as I folded the page and stood. "Thank you."

"My sister… When I last saw her, she was not well. They had taken her soul. There was nothing in her eyes, but she could care and she could love, and she would never ever want to hurt another girl as she had been hurt. I know this."

"Thanks again," I said and turned my back on her, then faced her again. "By the way…" I ripped a slit from the paper she'd given me and then took a pencil out of the holder. "Here's my number. Call me if you remember something else." As I wrote, I pretended as if I'd made a mishap and the pencil flew out of my hand, hit the file cabinet behind her, and landed on the floor.

When she bent down to pick it up, I snatched another one of the pencils with a chewed eraser out of the container and slipped it into my pocket.

"Sorry about that," I said, sort of smiling at her. I didn't want to lay it on too thick. "Not many people use pencils anymore."

"When I balance my books, I need the pencil to erase."

I wanted to ask why she didn't have software that could do it but decided it wasn't my business. I told her I understood, and this time when I made to leave, I actually left.

I walked rapidly up the short hallway and through the door. When Jada saw me, she jumped to her feet. I pointed my head toward the exit. There was no way in hell I was going to walk out first. The two guys whom she had struck up a conversation with said goodbye to her, and just about every guy in the establishment was watching her. I didn't like them staring at her that way. She was beautiful—that was for sure—and sexy as hell, but she was off the market as far as they were concerned.

Finally, she walked past me as I stood at the counter. I wanted to pull her against me and let her feel what she was doing to my cock, but I still had to be careful. Instead, I sighed hard, forcing my hands to stay off her. But there was one thing I was sure about. We were heading back to the airport and not a hotel room. Once we boarded my plane, we were going straight to bed. Her ass in those jeans... I watched it as she walked out the door and headed toward the car. I followed behind her, gnawing on my bottom lip, making plans to eat her ass and pussy until her body went weak from all the orgasms I was going to give her. Pleasure... That was what I was going to bring Jada Forte—total pleasure and never pain.

CHAPTER SEVEN

JADA FORTE

"Mmm-ah!" I cried and moaned. It was a high-pitched, unrestrained sound that came from deep in the back of my throat. I climaxed so hard my head could've hit the ceiling. And he still wasn't done. I had to look down at his head between my thighs several times to make sure Spencer was actually choosing to keep going. He had done things to me he'd never done before.

At that moment, I felt his soft tongue slide up the crack of my ass again. My eyes grew wide just as it had the first time he'd done it. Holy shit, I'd never thought a guy would ever do that to a woman. Then he flipped me over to tongue-fuck my pussy before latching on to my clit and making me come all over again. I hadn't known my body could experience that many orgasms. I'd stopped counting at seventeen or eighteen.

Spencer wasn't talking. The only sounds filling the cabin were my moaning, hissing, sucking air, and crying out intermingled with his licking, slurping, and grunting. There was also the ruffling of sheets, the noise of my fingernails digging into the mattress or the nearest pillow, and the creaking of the bed as Spencer stood me on my knees, flipped me on my back, or stretched my legs this way or that way. Frankly, it was the sexiest music I'd ever heard.

Holy hell, he was doing me like a starved lion. His tongue was building another orgasm inside me. My bottom half was so securely fastened against his mouth that I couldn't squirm away from the intense pleasure.

"Oh, Spencer, please…" I whispered, panting.

The fact that I said something seemed to make him even more voracious.

"Ah…" I nailed the back of my head against the mattress, nearly whiting out yet again as an orgasm streaked through my pussy.

Spencer muttered, "Fuck," and tried to guide

me onto my stomach for whatever he wanted to do to me next. This time, I put a hand against his chest as a sign of resistance.

"Babe, what?" I whispered, breathing heavily.

His eyes looked ravenous.

"What's going on? Why are you so horny?"

He had been acting strange ever since we left the café. When we were in the car, he made out with me all the way to the airport. I thought he would do me in the back seat, but instead he shoved his hand down my pants and rubbed me off a few times.

He had put his lips against my ear. "Don't mind the driver. I want to hear you tell me how good this feels," he said, then sank his tongue inside my ear. The erotic sensation made me moan even louder.

The airplane shook from turbulence, and Spencer seemed to not notice as he once again tried to guide me onto my stomach. I couldn't. One more orgasm and I would go blind or something.

I pressed my hands on both sides of his face. "Spencer, we have to call it off for a while. My body can't take any more. And what caused all of this in the first place?"

He stared into my eyes, blinking slowly. After a

few beats, he sighed. "I don't know. I can't stop wanting to taste you and hear you."

His hooded gaze made him look so sexy when he said that. If I wasn't so spent, I would've guided his face back to my pussy and said, "Taste away, baby."

"What about you?" I asked.

His eyes narrowed. "What about me?"

"Do you want me to do you?"

Spencer's head shook softly. "Not yet. But…"

He reached into one of the nightstands and retrieved a condom. I captured my bottom lip between my teeth as I watched him roll the rubber onto his engorged cock. I had to touch it, and when I wrapped my hand around his manhood, it was as solid as stone.

"Shit," I muttered.

He raised his eyebrows, letting me know he agreed with me. He was turned on beyond belief.

"If I don't fuck you, baby, then I'm going to have blue balls for months."

We both chuckled as he guided me back onto the bed, his strong body parting my thighs as his erection plunged into my pussy. Spencer and I had engaged in a lot of sex, but after all those orgasms I'd had, my insides were already sensitive. I had to hold onto him tight, gasping for air to withstand the intense pleasure.

Our mouths melted together, but our tongues and lips kept detaching so I could sigh or moan or bear the electricity his thrusts set off throughout my pussy. Finally, he increased his pumping. He grabbed the backboard, and I already knew what that meant. I clung to the sheets as he jabbed me one good, hard time, pinning the tip of his dick so deep inside me I could feel him in my belly.

Spencer threw his head back and yelled, "Shit!"

WE WERE ON OUR WAY TO PHOENIX. THE CAPTAIN had told us it was a four-hour-and-fifteen-minute flight. I could hardly believe it when he said we'd be landing in less than four hours. Spencer had been engaged in two-hundred variations of doing me since before we blasted down the runway. He now held me close against his sweat-soaked body.

"Sorry about all that, babe," he whispered and then his tongue drew circles around the hotspot on the back of my shoulder.

I shivered and he did it again.

"I think it was seeing all those guys wanting to fuck you but knowing they couldn't and I could."

I frowned. "What guys are you referring to?"

"The guys in the café."

I had no idea what he was talking about. The entire time I was seated at the table, I had been so nervous that I barely recognized who was around me.

"If anyone was getting eye service, it was you," I countered. "I mean, the waitress couldn't stop looking at you all starry-eyed. Oh," I said and then flipped around to face him. "I nearly died when she recognized you. Then everyone else heard her and started figuring out who you were too. I did whatever I could to take the attention off you."

He planted a quick and tender kiss on my lips. "I noticed."

My eyebrows lifted. "You did?"

"I did, baby."

We stared into each other's eyes. I wanted to be closer to him than I already was, but there would be no more sex until we both cooled off some. I broke eye contact when I remembered something. "Oh, so, I think I noticed something about Sarah or Nadia."

He frowned as if to say he was all ears.

"She has a prosthetic leg. Did you know that?"

Spencer looked at me incredulously. "What?"

"When I was in high school, my mom would drag me to Washington with her for the summer so I could"—I drew air quotes— "intern competitively, which meant whatever I did gave her the competitive edge, not me."

Spencer's scowl deepened. I'd forgotten that as far as my mom was concerned, I should watch my cynicism. I wasn't sure how long Spencer and I would last in a relationship. I hoped forever. And if forever, then my mom wasn't going anywhere. Disappearing into the background wasn't her style. He would have to deal with her for our eternity, so it behooved me to convince him to have a mere grain of respect for her. After all, a grain was all we both needed to tolerate her after the hospital fiasco.

I sighed to battle the intense desire to explain away my mother's self-centeredness. "Anyway, my first two summers, I worked at the veteran's hospital. There were lots of soldiers who had been fitted with prosthetics. No matter how naturally they could walk with their new appendage, I always noticed they all had the same sort of limp. Nadia has that limp even though she's really good at walking naturally."

Spencer flipped onto his back and scowled at the ceiling. "I didn't notice," he whispered as if he were scolding himself for missing it.

"You have to know what the walk looks like to notice it," I said.

He turned to face me and watched me with that thoughtful frown of his.

I rubbed my hand up and down his scrumptious chest. "What is it?"

He captured my hand by the wrist. "Babe…" He swallowed hard. "I'm still primed for fucking. Are you?"

I stretched my mouth squeamishly and pulled my hand out of his gentle grasp.

We both chuckled softly. I was seriously tired of climaxing, and there had only been a few times when Spencer's been inside me and hadn't stimulated me to full-on orgasm. It was so different than what I had heard about sex before I started having it. My friends would talk a lot about faking it and getting themselves off when the guy fell asleep because she wanted an orgasm so badly. I made a mental note to talk to Hope about all the orgasms Spencer had given me. Was his dick made of magic? Or was climaxing just about every time he was fucking me the norm? Hope would know.

"Listen…" he said, making his tone serious. "I want to tell you something."

I made my expression as somber as his. "I'm listening."

"The only parts of Irina excavated from the wall were her right fibula, tibia, and foot."

I took a moment to fully put the pieces together. "Wait." I propped myself up. "Are you saying Nadia could be Irina?"

Spencer scratched the side of his head. "I don't know. Nestor, my investigator, is keeping an eye on her. He suspects she'll try to run after my visit. When I was in her office, she had a lot of pencils with erasers that had been chewed on. I managed to lift one from her. As soon as we land, we'll stop somewhere, and I'll overnight it to Nestor for DNA testing."

I nodded continuously. "So this Irina woman could link Arthur Valentine to the dead bodies?"

Spencer propped himself up. "I don't know what she knows. I only remember overhearing Valentine ask my father if he handled Irina just as he had all the girls that were found in the wall."

My neck jutted forward as my eyes expanded. "Wow." I didn't know what else to say.

"I was young when I heard it, so…" He

sounded as if he were speaking in defense of why he hadn't exposed the two men when he had initially heard them talk about what they had done to the girls.

I shook my head. "Spencer, you have nothing to feel guilty or ashamed of."

His eyebrows pulled toward the bridge of his nose, stayed there for a while, and evened out.

Spencer gulped. "I know. You're right." He started shaking his head. "But the more I think about it, the more I'm questioning whether or not there's been a puppeteer pulling my strings."

"What do you mean?" I asked.

He flipped onto his back again and glared at the ceiling as if addressing it. "My investigator gets through to the grandmother, who tells me Irina has a sister who lives in Toronto. We would have to assume that if Nadia is actually Irina, then the grandmother would've known it."

This time when I rubbed his chest, he didn't stop me. "You're right."

It fell silent between us.

"What do you think she has locked away in Phoenix?" I asked.

He reached into the nightstand to get another condom. "I don't know, babe."

This time it was me who seized his wrist. "You know we don't need that."

He tilted his head curiously.

"I'm on birth control."

His mouth fell open. "When?"

"I had it taken care of when we were on our break."

Spencer's frown grew more intense. "Why?"

I told him about the small scare I had. My period had come three days late, which was something that never happened. My monthly was like clockwork. So I'd got worried and went to Dr. Nancy, who had been treating me since high school, for a pregnancy test. She carefully informed me I would have to wait a little longer to know if I was pregnant or not, but if my monthly came, then she would recommend birth control. The next day my monthly came. It lasted its usual three days and then, a week later, I got birth control.

Spencer tossed the condom back in the drawer. "Shit, and you're just now telling me?"

He was mounting me and separating my thighs. "Well—" I gasped as he drove his erection deep inside me.

"By the way, baby." He sucked air, then sank his tongue in my ear.

My body shivered. "Um hmm…" I said, moaning.

"I want you to marry me."

My eyes popped open to full expansion as Spencer thrust his erection in and out of me, slowly, indulgently, muttering about how good I felt.

CHAPTER EIGHT

JADA FORTE

Spencer came hard. We made out and slept a little. The captain announced we would be landing in fifteen minutes, so Spencer took the opportunity to wipe me clean as he usually did. Then we dressed ourselves and went to sit in the seats in the front cabin and strapped ourselves in for landing. He hadn't mentioned the marriage part again, and I didn't bring it up either. The girls in my circle knew the rule was if he said he loved you while fucking you, then it didn't count. I imagined the same went for proposing while fucking too.

We ran into a bit of a snafu when we tried to hit the ground running in Phoenix. The car Spencer had ordered to meet us in front of the terminal wasn't there and he nearly lost his head, demanding the service got someone to the airport to pick us up pronto. I'd never seen him behave so "entitled" before. I thought it had something to do with him wanting to take back the proposal of marriage he'd made to me while inside me. I stood beside him quietly, pressing my lips, trying to keep my bearings intact. Then he called Clyde, the vice president of his company, and stepped away from me to have a conversation with him.

I stood alone, debating whether to call Hope or not. I decided to wait because I wanted to be in an environment where I could speak freely to her. However, I didn't have to stand there alone and feeling lonely for long. Our car pulled up and Spencer opened the door to let me in, then he got in after the driver put our luggage in the trunk. He was on the phone with Nestor as we headed to the UPS store. Spencer told his investigator what I had noticed about Nadia's leg. I was glad he happily gave me credit for it. That was when I thought perhaps I was being overly sensitive and that he wasn't angry because he accidentally asked me to marry him.

I was now waiting for him in the car while he was inside the UPS Store to mail off the pencil. He'd been in there for a while, and when I saw one excited person after the next hurrying out of the establishment, I knew what was keeping him. Spencer Christmas, one of the richest men in the world, son of the fallen but redeemed by his acts of valor, was in the store. People were probably asking for autographs and selfies. I sighed with relief when I saw him walk out the door. The corners of my mouth pulled downward when I saw two chicks flanking him while smiling up at him. Their skinny jeans were so tight that their legs looked like skinny toothpicks—and their platinum blond hair stretched down to their asses.

I wondered if walking out with those women was further proof that Spencer was letting me know he had made a mistake by asking me to marry him. I crossed my arms, huffing as I ripped my eyes off the three of them.

He had some nerve flirting with those attention-starved bimbos in front of me. I dared not to look at him as he got into the car. If I had then, I would've exploded with anger, so I kept my focus on the downtown storefronts.

"Are you hungry?" he asked.

"Yes," I said, continuing to look out the window even though I was unable to discern much of what I was seeing.

"Are you okay?" he asked.

Then, as if my anger blossomed through me like a plume of toxic smoke, I whipped my face in his direction. "You don't have to treat me this way, you know."

He jerked his head backward. "Treat you what way?"

"Don't play dumb with me. You know you're freezing me out. If you want to take back what you said on the plane, then fine. Do it. I didn't take you seriously in the first place. A proposal while fucking doesn't count." I was so angry that I was breathing through my nostrils like an angry bull.

He closed his eyes gravely and then after a moment cleared his throat. "I meant it, Jada," he said in a passionate whisper.

The three words he just spoke took my breath away as my mouth fell open. Finally, I swallowed. "You did?"

"But you ignored me. I thought it was your way of saying no."

I tried to play back the moment when he had asked. He was fucking me. I was shocked.

"But you didn't stop and wait for my reply?"

"Well..." he said, raising his forehead. "You

looked petrified as hell. I thought I'd wait for you to say something first, but you never did."

I squished one side of my face. "How could a confident, sexy man like you, Spencer Christmas, assume I would reject your proposal?"

"Jada..." He scooted closer to me, and now our lips were close enough to kiss. "I try to be a confident man, but at times that's difficult. But I saw panic in your eyes, baby, and you can't deny it."

After a moment of watching him pensively, I sighed. I had to admit the truth. "Yes, of course the idea of marriage scares the living daylights out of me. I mean, my parents were never as close as we are now."

"Your parents were business partners, not lovers."

I turned my head slightly. "You sound sure of that."

His eyes narrowed. "Aren't you?"

I closed my eyes and forced my brain to come up with an answer from deep inside my consciousness. "Yes."

"Open your eyes, baby," he whispered.

I did as he asked, and now our gazes were connected.

"I love you, Jada. You're just meant for me.

That's all. I want to be married to you. Will you marry me?"

I opened my mouth to answer, but I couldn't come up with a response. Marriage? I wasn't even thirty yet. Spencer was the first guy I'd ever had sex with. I hadn't even had my career figured out.

"Forget it," he said. "You're right. Maybe we should fucking forget I ever asked."

My mouth wouldn't close and words still wouldn't form. I was trapped in indecision. Finally, I cleared my throat.

"I'm more patient than you are," I said.

"What the fuck does that mean?" he asked curtly.

"I always give you time to finish what you're saying or feeling but you never give me time." That wasn't true of course, but it felt like it in the moment.

"Do you need time to give me an answer?" His tone was curious and patient.

"Yes," I said without hesitation.

Spencer studied me thoughtfully. I decided to not wait for him to complete his deliberation process to further convince him to grant my request.

I shifted my body to face him. "I believe you

love me because I'm independent and self-sufficient. I've been banging my head against the bricks ever since graduating from college. I've been surviving, really. Then I met you. And…" I sighed and rolled my neck wearily. Was I making any sense at all? I had to pull my thoughts together better than I was.

"Take your time, Jada," Spencer said.

I grunted as I smiled. My tender, patient, and loving Spencer seemed to be back. And now without feeling the pressure of saying something before I lost his attention, my thoughts became clear as a bell.

"Once one of my friends presented me with this theory of surviving and thriving," I said. "She said most people turn thirty, forty, fifty, sixty, and sometimes they're one hundred years old and never enter the thriving mode of life. I want to know who I am. I want to thrive. It's why I moved far away from my mom, but it never stopped her from pulling me into her toolbox whenever she needed me to fix something for her. That was me surviving. When I went to Santa Barbara against the advice of everyone who watched my mom through lenses I didn't possess, that was me surviving as well."

I had said a lot and now my eyes were full of tears, not sad tears though, happy ones.

Spencer took me by the hands. "Babe, you don't have to anymore. I understand. I'll wait." He shifted his body abruptly to face me. "How about this? Forget I ever asked you to marry me."

I felt my expression drop into sadness as I moaned.

Spencer made his sexy smirk as he leaned in closer to me. "I will ask you to marry me again. As far as I'm concerned, you're the only woman for me, but I want to do it right. Not while fucking you."

We both chuckled at the veiled humor in that.

"I want to do it right in every way," he said. "Will you allow me the opportunity?"

"I will," I said and threw my arms around his neck. My tongue lapped up his and then they swirled around each other. The fact that I initiated our kiss, probably for the first time ever, hadn't been lost on me. Perhaps it was because Spencer had a way of needing to control our touching, kissing, and fucking. I had always believed if he wasn't in charge, then he felt violated. But here he was, accepting my kiss. Of course he'd taken over and was lowering me down onto the seat, kissing me as if there was no tomorrow. But the fact that I had initiated our contact made me even hornier than I was two seconds ago.

"Sir, we've arrived," the driver said. His tone had hit a nervous high note.

He must've heard me unzip Spencer's pants. Now, Spencer and I were staring at each other with a burning passion. He must've known I was going to sink his cock all the way into my mouth. It was time I tasted him. If I was going to be his wife, then he would have to grant me permission to blow him whenever and wherever I wanted.

I zipped up his pants and put a kiss on his parted lips.

"Next time," I whispered.

He raised an eyebrow. I kept my curious expression fixated on him. He swallowed hard and then nodded.

It took Spencer a few moments to cool off and figure out that the first number Nadia had written was the gate access code. We were now chasing the second number, which was building number twenty-three and unit number 1507. Spencer and I walked down a long, silent hallway past metal doors, our legs still wobbly from our last make-out session in the back seat of the car.

"Shit, I'm getting blue balls," he said, adjusting his big dick in his pants.

I believed him and was about to suggest I could relieve him when he announced we had arrived. We were standing in front of an orange metal door. Then he gave me the page, and I read aloud the numbers to the combination, which he opened the lock with on the first try.

Serious Spencer was back in full force as he squatted to yank up the door. Our reactions were stuck in awe as we took in the bloody chainsaws and axes, loads of brown boxes, and one long table.

Suddenly, Spencer's arm shot in front of me, gesturing for me to stay put. He took out his phone and called his investigator, who told us to wait. The appropriate law enforcement authorities would arrive soon.

I couldn't rip my eyes away from our discovery. The storage was air-conditioned, which did a lot to contain the mild sulfuric scent of aging blood. Then I spotted something that looked out of place and pointed at it.

"That doesn't look like it should be here," I said.

Spencer glared at the fresh, bright-white envelope sitting on top of one of the boxes. He crossed his own barrier that he had mentally erected to get it. "It has my name on it."

We stared at each other for a few wonderstruck seconds, then he cautiously opened the unsealed envelope. Spencer took out what appeared to be a thick letter and read to himself. I stood with my arms crossed, feeling anxious. I wanted so much to hear the words on the paper but knew it was up to Spencer whether he wanted to share them.

It felt like it took him forever to read what was written, but then he looked at me. "We got him, babe." He sighed as if he'd just shrugged the world off his shoulders. "We got him."

CHAPTER NINE

JADA FORTE

S pencer had given all but two pages of the letter to the authorities, who swarmed the scene like ants on candy. Before the first news team had showed up, Spencer had already made some calls and soon I was in the back of the car alone, heading to an estate he said I would love in Scottsdale.

"I want you to relax, unwind, and try to forget what you've seen here," he said. "I'll be there later."

I said I would try, and my answer was good enough for him. Spencer kissed me and made sure I was tucked away safely within the confines of the vehicle before closing the car door. I felt a terrible sense of anxiety about leaving him behind. So much had happened within the last forty-eight hours that I had to massage my temples to slow the spinning sensation inside my head when I thought about it all.

The good thing was the closer we got to Scottsdale, the more majestic the landscapes turned beyond my window. The sprawling desert with its naturally placed rocks and arid plant life made up the sort of views I would normally stop to capture on my phone's camera if I were on a vacation. The higher we headed along the inclining road, the prettier the cacti, rock formations, and plants were. I wanted to find a trail and hike through it, but the desire abandoned me almost as soon as it had come. My life was in shambles. There was no way I could start enjoying living until all my shit was in order.

Finally, the car stopped in front of a large decorative wrought-iron gate. The driver punched a code into the keypad and the panel rolled open, and we drove onto the property. A field of feathery trees surrounded by white rocks layered the grounds to my left. Pathways lined by ground lamps curved through the landscape. Also, the quaint, black iron benches posted throughout caught my eye.

To my right was a terrain of bright-green grass inlaid with the same walkways, which lay in circular patterns surrounding a great bowl-shaped fountain that spurted water.

However, the closer we got to the modern mansion, made mostly of white stone with wide and tall windows and doors, the more the construct demanded all eyes on it. With the mountains rising behind it, the property felt like a real retreat, which was why my body instantly let go of the tension it'd been holding.

The car rolled to a stop on smooth red stone which spread past an opened black iron gate and all the way to the base of the front steps.

Excited, I opened my door at the same time the driver opened his. The trunk popped, and I stepped around to retrieve my suitcase.

I reached for my luggage. "I'll take mine."

"No, Miss Forte. The house staff will handle that for you," he said.

Being treated as if I were perpetually on an all-inclusive vacation at a five-star resort was something I wasn't sure I'd ever get used to. However, I smiled at the driver, said thanks, and trotted toward the massive wooden door, which opened before I reached it. I boldly entered, then stopped under the high-coffered ceilings to get an eyeful of the environment around me. The wide, open spaces I could see contained beautiful chandeliers and pristine modern furniture that supported the minimalistic but elegant design style.

"Good evening, Miss Forte," a woman said in the most welcoming tone.

I ripped my gaze from the opulence around me and set it on two women standing to my left, who were wearing maid uniforms. I was no longer shocked by people knowing my name before I arrived. It was part of the billionaire treatment, and if I said yes to Spencer's proposal, I would probably have to start getting used to the invasive aspect of his lifestyle.

One of the women said she would show me to "your and Mr. Christmas's room." I followed her up a flight of curving stairs to the second floor, beaming because I loved how she had called the space we were heading to mine and Spencer's. It made me feel even more so like we were a solid couple.

The hallway nearly took my breath away, especially as I looked through the glass wall on one side of us which showcased the lights of town in the valley below. The drive up to the estate felt so even that I hadn't noticed how high up we'd ascended.

I kept saying wow, and the maid turned to show

me her smiling profile. We made it to the bedroom, and the layout and design of the space nearly took my breath away. First, I spotted the aqua-blue waters of a lit swimming pool. It was beyond a sitting area that contained a white leather sectional with a large square ottoman and an unlit electric fireplace encased in a blocky glass pillar, which served the sleek décor and grabbed my special attention. Then, all of a sudden, I noticed chaises, the chandelier above the king-sized bed, and the accent wall made of tufted silver sheets of metal behind the bed. I'd never seen anything like the room.

I touched myself on the chest. "This is a very beautiful home."

"Yes, it is, Miss Forte," the maid said.

I stopped myself from stepping into the room after noticing its thick, off-white carpet. The fibers were the sort which made the bottoms of feet feel as if they were walking on a cloud. Right away, I unzipped and snatched off my booties and socks one foot at a time.

"I will take those," the maid said.

I halted my excitement to examine her. Conforming to the nature of my environment hadn't rubbed off on me yet. My mom may have

113

committed a lot of unscrupulous acts, but she had made sure it was ingrained in me to never treat anyone as if it were their job to serve me.

I touched the maid gently on her small shoulder. "I'm sorry, I never got your name."

Her hospitable but emotionally distant smile was very much one that reminded me she was simply here to do her job and not be my friend. "I'm Lourdes, Miss Forte."

I quickly removed my hand. "Lourdes." I made my smile invitingly warm. "I can take care of my own shoes."

"Whatever you like, Miss Forte," she said.

"And please, call me Jada." That request was non-negotiable.

She made an obligatory nod. "Yes, Jada. Where would you like dinner to be served? We have the dining room…"

Finally I stepped onto the carpet, and just as I had expected, the fibers felt supple against my feet. "Up here if that's okay."

She said that was fine and then said my luggage was being unpacked and my things put away in the dresser and bathroom. I hadn't seen anyone bring my luggage into our room, but I wasn't surprised there was another secret entrance. I was beginning to wonder if the Christmases could live without pathways to skulk through. The thought would've bothered me when I had first met Spencer and then read the book about the family, but not anymore. I accepted and innately understood all facets of Spencer Christmas as he had mine.

Lourdes also showed me where the bathroom was, which was another space that also deserved an applause for its opulence. She then directed me where to find the swim wear and told me the pool was warm. Her final instruction to me was that dinner would be surf and turf with filet mignon and would be served within the hour.

I felt as if I should've tipped her or something, but instead, I made sure my expression conveyed how much I appreciated her kindness and attention. As soon as I was alone, I undressed, taking off everything, including my underwear, and fell on top of the bed. For some reason, I felt released from whatever unknown thing that had had me bound. What just occurred between Lourdes and me was a reason I had hesitated when Spencer asked me to marry him. He was a real billionaire —like the real thing. I didn't know if I wanted to live his lifestyle. Didn't he ever just want to be free? It felt natural being stuck on a subway during rush hour or grabbing a banana and a cup of coffee from the first food cart I saw because I didn't have time to whip up a bowl of oatmeal for breakfast. Didn't Spencer want to spend an entire Saturday cleaning his house, washing his clothes, and getting caught up on all the TV shows he'd missed during the week because he'd been working too late and hanging with friends afterward, well beyond a reasonable bedtime? I did. Of course, half of that wasn't possible with living in a house the size of the one I was in. Even his New York penthouse was too large to clean in one day. The apartment I used to live in before moving to Wyoming to work for Spencer was bite-sized. It was mine though. I paid the rent. My name was on the lease.

Then, suddenly struck by illumination, I sat up. I had been stuck in college-aged, not-yet-quite-a-full-adult Jada for a long time. However, all of that had changed the moment I accepted Spencer's job and moved into his ranch house. It was that one life transition that had made me who I was today. I had been sure it was how life would continue to unfold. Could I continue to grow and evolve if I married a man who had the world at his fingertips? Or would I have to feel as if life wasn't moving in the right direction unless I spent each day slugging through shit?

I turned toward the swimming pool. Narrowing my eyes at the blue waters did something to me on the inside. I asked myself, What would an uninhibited Jada do? Without taking another moment to figure out the answer, I stood and trotted to the large French door, which to my surprise automatically slid open when I got close enough. After my amazement passed, I picked up speed again, and the next thing I knew, naked as a jaybird, I leapt off the edge of the pool. I purposely chose to not perform a perfect dive, an act that would've made my mother proud, especially if I had done it in front of all the people she wanted to impress. Nope, I tucked my legs against my chest, wrapped my arms around them, and hit the water in the form of a cannonball.

SPENCER MUST'VE KNOWN THAT AS SOON AS I HAD arrived at the mansion, I would lose myself. Time slipped by as I swam laps, floated on my back, and swam deep underwater. After a dive that would've made my mother gloat shamelessly about how well

I had been trained to swim, my stomach growled. I grabbed on to the edge of the pool to peer into the bedroom beyond the window and saw dinner had been set up on a round table, which sat between the sitting and sleeping areas.

Famished, I lifted myself out of the water, my body dripping wet.

"Good Lord, shit," I heard Spencer say.

I whipped my face toward the far end area of the patio. Spencer was standing there. The tired way which his shoulders slumped and the sweat glistening across his face were telltale signs of how worn-out he was. However, the ravenous look in his eyes told a different story.

CHAPTER TEN

JADA FORTE

S pencer extended an arm, pointing at me. "Don't fucking move an inch." His voice cracked, so he cleared his throat.

First, he pulled his shirt off over his head. Next, he unbuttoned and took off his pants. When his underwear came off, my eyes expanded at his engorged cock.

"Do you have the energy to do this?" I asked.

He really looked tired.

Spencer cracked a slight smirk. "No. but…" He made it to me and lowered his head to suck as much of my right breast into the concaves of his warm, wet mouth as he could.

"Mmm," he said, grabbing my nipple gently

between his teeth and shaking his head, tugging it back and forth.

My body quickened as I sucked air, feeling the stinging and tingling sensation.

"Just don't move," he whispered and then did it again.

I moved.

He shoved his fingers into my pussy and pulled my body against his. Then he put his lips on my ear.

"I said don't move," he whispered and raked his teeth across my earlobes.

I moaned, trying to comply, as he nibbled all the hot spots on my neck and then moved to his and my favorites on the back of my shoulder.

"I need to fuck you. No frills. Just fuck. Will you let me?" he whispered.

I closed my eyes to sip air between my teeth. That sounded so sexy. I nodded stiffly, trembling from anticipation. Suddenly his thumb was smashing and rounding my clit. The sensations struck me like a sudden downpour of rain. When I threw my arms around his neck, his lips pressed against mine and his tongue sank into my mouth and whirled around mine.

Spencer lifted my feet off the ground. I

wrapped my legs around his waist as he carried me. When he put me down, we were still on the patio and next to a wrought iron cocktail table. He quickly turned me around and used his foot to spread my feet wide. Then he guided my belly onto the tabletop.

"Hold on tight, baby," he whispered. His voice was laced with pure lust.

As he clutched my hips, I held on tightly to the edge of the table. I was curious about what was going to come next when he lifted my lower body as if I were light as a feather.

"Ah!" I cried as his cock soared into my pussy.

"Ha!" Spencer said, banging me hard. With each nailing of his dick deep inside me, he roared.

He fucked me hard, and I felt his tip hitting the bottom of my pussy as his hands squeezed my flesh. Then after one hard jab, he let out a resounding roar and swept me off the table and held my back against him while shaking with orgasm.

We both breathed heavily as we stood still for a moment.

"I hope that didn't make you feel dirty," he said.

I gulped as I shook my head. "Not at all."

He kissed and nibbled the hot spot on the back of my shoulder, and I shivered. "Good, because I liked doing you that way without feeling like a fucking animal."

He gently took himself out of me and softly put my feet back on the concrete. I turned to face him and we kissed. My head did some light spinning as I whispered, "You can fuck me like an animal any time you want."

Our mouths chuckled against each other.

My stomach growled loud and long.

Spencer frowned. "You were hungry?"

I shrugged indifferently. "Yeah, but I'd rather have you"—I flexed my eyebrows twice— "than food."

He kissed me deeply again before leading me into the bathroom to dry all the way off. We both put on robes and dove into the surf and turf.

AS WE SAT ACROSS FROM EACH OTHER, SPENCER caught me up on what happened at the storage unit. In the two pages Spencer had not handed to the authorities, Irina confessed she was Nadia. The bulk of the pages in the envelope contained detailed explanations of the evidence in the storage unit, including names and addresses of witnesses who could shed some light on the investigation. Irina also asked Spencer to only hand over the letter to the authorities if he could keep her safe from Valentine's retaliation. Keeping Irina's request in mind, Spencer handed over the portion of the letter that dealt with the evidence to the FBI.

Most of the evidence incriminated Randolph Christmas. The evidence that led directly to Arthur Valentine were videotapes, audio recordings, and ledgers for shipping containers signed by him simply because at times he needed to throw his weight around and show up at a port to make a customs investigator release a shipping container. Irina, who had admittedly gone from fucking Valentine to working for him, had an inside person who was supposed to destroy all paperwork pertaining to their shipments. She'd never had any of them destroyed. They were all in a box, even the ones Valentine signed.

"Tomorrow, we're going to the lab to take a look at some videotapes too," he said.

My neck jutted forward from shock. "What? You're going to include me?"

He smirked while shaking his head. "No, babe, this is nothing you need to concern yourself with. Company is on the way."

My eyebrows merged into a curious frown. "Company?"

"My brother Jasper and his wife."

I nearly plopped to the edge of my seat. "Holly Henderson? The woman who wrote the book?"

Spencer nodded silently. "She wants the exclusive."

"Oh," I said curiously. "She still works as a journalist even though she's living the billionaire life?"

"Of course, Jada. It's her job, and she likes it." His eyes narrowed some more. "Do you think if you're married to me, you'll be forced to give up on your dreams?"

I sighed as I slumped in my seat. "The problem is I don't even know what to dream. I thought I liked PR, but I can clearly see my mom pushed me into the field because she wanted me to do that while residing in Patricia's world."

He grunted thoughtfully.

"Why the humph?" I asked.

Spencer shrugged indifferently. "My father wanted me in business for his benefit. Even though he disappointed the fuck out of me every day of my life, I still like what I do."

I studied Spencer, feeling as if I was looking

past his visible self to see into his soul. My brain was making sense out of what he'd just said.

"I liked working for Jimmy," I admitted.

"You did?" he roared, looking as if he were chewing on lemons.

I chuckled. "No... I didn't like Jimmy. He's a douche. I liked the work. I would've loved working for a candidate I could believe in." I turned my head slightly and grinned lopsided. "Like you."

Spencer's eyes smoldered. "That face you're showing me, could you do it again when we get in bed?"

I rolled my eyes and grunted. "Okay, then you're going to ignore my indirect proposal?"

He threw his hands up. "I'm sorry. What sort of response were you looking for?"

"I think you should run against Jimmy. You both are residents of Rhode Island and—"

"I'm not a resident of Rhode Island. I'm a California resident."

I gasped. "Get the fuck out of here, really? How? You don't live in California."

"No," he said, dipping his head as he easily conceded to that. "I never got around to changing my residency to New York after my father died. He made us all take up residencies in key states. Jasper's

New York, I'm California, and Asher's Texas. Only Bryn is Rhode Island."

I nodded energetically. "Right, in the book it says your father wanted Jasper to be the president, but he didn't have political aspirations for you, did he?"

"I was the backup plan." He tilted his head jerkily as he contemplated something. "I never said that out loud, and the thought used to make me, you know, feel pretty shitty."

I raised my eyebrows. "You don't feel shitty anymore?"

He shook his head as he pulled the corners of his mouth downward. "No. Not at all."

I smiled. "Then good for you."

We smoldered at each other for a long moment.

"I'm glad I'm here with you," he finally said.

"Same," I said, smiling.

I leaned across the table, leading with my lips, and his lips enthusiastically met mine in the middle. Our tongues brushed lightly at first and then fervently.

"Mmm…" He moaned and then sat back, breaking mouth contact. "My dick's run out of steam for now." Then Spencer did something I'd never seen him do. He yawned.

AFTER DINNER, WE WENT STRAIGHT TO BED. Spencer wrapped me up in his arms, and within minutes, he was asleep. At first I wanted to drift off, but then he started snoring, and all I could do was indulge in the sound. I tried to remember if there was ever a time when he had fallen asleep before I had. I racked my brain trying to find one instance. I couldn't. It had never happened. After a while, I kissed his face and he let go of me to roll over and ball into a fetal position. I'd never seen him do that either.

Suddenly I was wide awake and fighting the urge to go for another swim or take a long hot bath in the exquisite tub. However, the need to remain near Spencer was the victor, and I figured out how to get the TV to roll down from the ceiling before watching BCN news. I gasped when my mother's mug shot filled the screen. I glanced toward Spencer, but he was still sawing logs.

I turned up the volume and my jaw dropped farther. I listened to Stan Rochester of the Rochester Report say that my mother had been released on bond and claims she had no idea her campaign was taking money from foreign adversaries. In the next clip, my mom was glaring at the camera saying, "I'm appalled by this. And if I actually did it, then I should rightfully be carried off in handcuffs. But I didn't. And as a matter of fact," she said, pointing her finger fervently, "it's about time we finally commit ourselves to getting big money out of politics."

I didn't believe a word she said, but I was sure a lot of people did. Knowing my mother, she was on a full-fledged PR tour, and now my father and his son would be safe from her bitter ire. I had never asked my father about Stefan's mother. Whomever she was, I hoped he loved her.

The show had evolved to the roundtable portion of the program. Stan Rochester was at a table with my mother's political allies and enemies, discussing the veracity of her claim to not have known about the illegal donations.

Curt Twinning, the representative from Texas, was calling bullshit on her. Sally Gaines, a representative from Oregon, expertly led the name-calling and accusations into a discussion about how most of Congress were too busy to read the books, but if they were all put on the table, then three-quarters of the Senate and the House, if not all, would be arrested.

It was at that point I rolled my eyes and clicked off the television. As soon as the back of my head flopped against the pillow, Spencer curled an arm around me, guided me against him, and rubbed his burgeoning erection against my ass until it was full grown and inside me. We made love, and I didn't bring up what I'd heard on the Rochester Report, even though I wanted to.

CHAPTER ELEVEN

JADA FORTE

"Ah!" I cried as the sound of the doorbell chiming projected throughout our room.

It was morning. Spencer had woken up and kissed my mouth and down my neck. His tongue now lapped my nipple. He bit it, then kissed down my belly until he licked my clit. This was the third time I came, and I believed he was going for a repeat performance of what he'd done to me during our flight from Toronto to Phoenix, but the bell had interrupted him.

Spencer flopped onto his back and sighed gravely. "Shit. They're here."

THE BEDROOM HAD JACK AND JILL BATHROOMS, SO to stay focused, Spencer and I showered and prepared ourselves separately. As I finished blow-drying my hair in front of the mirror, the sun flowing into the dressing area through the large French doors beckoned me to step onto the patio to let the rays touch my skin, so I did. I raised my arms, letting the heat kiss my nakedness. It must've been eighty-one or eighty-two degrees out, the perfect temperature. I closed my eyes and directed my face toward the sunlight. Ever since I had started dating Spencer, I found myself uninhibited in the strangest ways. Before, I would've never risked someone catching me standing on the patio naked. When we were back at the ranch and in the early stages of fucking all the time, whenever the servers would walk into the room, I would shriek under the covers and hide my face. But now, at this very moment, I didn't care if they perceived Spencer and I had been having sex.

I took one last deep breath in through my nostrils and went back inside to finish up. If I had known I'd end up in Arizona, I would've packed cooler and prettier clothes, like a sundress or two, but all I had were the standard jeans, sweaters, and a few long- and short-sleeved shirts to wear under my sweaters.

Regardless, I put on a pair of jeans and my light-blue, aged cotton T-shirt and headed to the bedroom to meet Spencer. When I entered, he was sitting on the sofa, typing something on his cell phone.

"I'm ready," I announced.

He snapped his attention in my direction and shot to his feet. "Wow," he said, his eyebrows lifted. "You look good."

Spencer had on a pair of heather-gray slacks that fit his athletic body like a glove and an aqua-blue T-shirt. I loved that about him, the fact that he was the kind of man who didn't shy away from wearing color.

"You do too," I said, not breaking stride as I walked toward him.

When I got close enough, he guided me against him and we kissed.

"Are you matching me on purpose?" he asked with a sexy smirk on his face.

I pressed the tip of my finger against his hard chest. "I think it was you"—I stabbed my own chest — "who copied me."

This time when we kissed, we almost went too far, but Spencer forced his mouth off mine.

"Let's get the hell out of here or else," he said with a sigh.

I flexed my eyebrows twice. "Let's," I said past the frog in my throat.

We would've kissed again, but Spencer took me by the hand and we walked off, heading to the dining room for breakfast with his brother, sister-in-law, and the niece Spencer would be meeting for the first time.

I DIDN'T THINK CHRISTMAS COULD BE EVEN merrier until I laid eyes on Spencer's brother Jasper. My goodness, he was a sight to behold. It wasn't that he was more handsome than Spencer— because in my book he wasn't. They were equally handsome, but each in his own way. Spencer was more athletic and had the good looks of an exotic-looking male model. Jasper was maybe two inches taller and resembled a classically handsome A-list actor. Also, Jasper's eyes were a shade of blue I'd never seen before, and they looked striking against his all-black outfit. He struck me as a man who rarely wore color. It wasn't that he had a heavy disposition, but he exuded a seriousness that not even Spencer, who was a very serious person, could match. Our official greeting began with a tight handshake and then progressed into a hesitant hug. He smelled good but his scent was not as delicious as Spencer's.

"It's nice to finally meet you, Jada," he said while scowling. If I hadn't spent so much time around Spencer, with that look on Jasper's face, I wouldn't have believed him.

"Nice to meet you as well," I said, sounding overly formal.

Finally, I turned toward the other woman in the room. "Holly, I presume?" I asked, mirroring the huge smile she was showing me. Her beautiful daughter, who had her father's sea-blue eyes, was sitting on her lap digging her little hand in scrambled eggs and stuffing what she was able to retrieve from her plate into her mouth.

Holly nodded graciously. "I would stand, but…"

The little girl shook her hands like a rattle, speaking baby gibberish, and then laughed. Then something that appeared as if it could have been miraculous happened. Jasper's entire face lit up as he laughed. Spencer watched his brother with confusion. One thing was for sure. Jasper really loved his daughter, who was certainly a happy baby.

My chuckle simmered, and I raised a hand to let Holly know there was no need to get up. "It's okay."

"There's Uncle Spencer," Holly said to the little girl, who studied Spencer in awe.

I leaned toward the baby and whispered, "That was my reaction too when I first saw him."

Holly laughed, and I was positive she was the only person who got my joke.

Soon we all settled at the table and the servers gave us all blueberry, strawberry, and lemon crème crepes and fresh fruit. Spencer and I sat beside each other on one side of the table and Jasper and Holly on the other. Holly went right into her pitch on why she thought she was the best person to tell Irina's story.

"Although," she said and then looked at Jasper with raised eyebrows. Right on cue, Jasper reached his hands toward his daughter, Jane, who nearly sprang into his arms.

"Although what?" Spencer asked impatiently. There was something about Holly that seemed to irritate him and then I recalled Bryn saying something to the effect that in me, Spencer had found his own version of Holly.

She ran a hand through her illustrious dark locks, agitated her scalp, and sighed as she sat up straight. "So, a week ago my guy in the lab came clean about something."

"Came clean about what?" Spencer asked tersely.

"When I collected your family's DNA—"

"Without any of our permission," Spencer said.

I turned to look at him, surprised by how rude he was being toward her. His jaw was set. It was strange, and I was starting to wonder if he had a crush on her. Holly Christmas was stunning—that was for sure—with her dark hair, doe eyes, naturally red mouth, and flawless skin. She obviously didn't have to work hard to accentuate any of her assets.

Spencer's eyes darted in my direction and then he readjusted in his seat.

"Right, yes, but in all fairness, I was just doing my job, so…" Holly winked at him. "Not apologizing, so get over it."

Spencer pressed his lips slightly. He quickly glanced at me, then set a glare that matched his brother's back on her.

His expression was colder than polar icecaps. "What else?"

She leaned back just an inch or two. "Jasper will take it from here, and I promise, Spencer, this is going to have a happy ending." Holly stood and signaled Jasper to hand over Jane. After they made the exchange, she announced she was taking Jane upstairs to a nanny named September and would be right back.

"What is it, Jasper?" Spencer asked once the sleeping child was out of the room.

His gaze meandered somewhere beyond our heads. "She didn't sleep well. Jane has difficulties sleeping on airplanes," he said as if he were speaking to himself. Then, Jasper abruptly leaned forward, directing his body toward Spencer. "Spence, Asher, Bryn, and I have DNA profiles that come up whenever we submit our samples for DNA testing. Our info is inaccurate on purpose."

Spencer snarled. "Dad?"

Jasper looked so much like Spencer when he pursed his lips and nodded in response.

"I sent Nestor the DNA report that Holly's contact had completed. Her guy never put our name in the universal database since he ran our

DNA without consent. Therefore, her readings are accurate."

I contained my exclamation to what Jasper had just revealed. I remembered reading in the book that the siblings' DNA had been confirmed but there was a footnote explaining that the samples were acquired by undisclosed methods as to protect all those involved. I now knew the truth, which made me feel as if I had landed securely in the middle of the Christmases' inner circle.

Spencer's mouth was caught open, and I could tell his brain was working overtime processing the same conclusion I had already come to.

"Then some of the remains found could still belong to my mother."

"Yes," Jasper said.

I gently bit my lip as Spencer and I made strong eye contact. After a few beats, he took a deep breath and then faced his brother again. Jasper explained that Holly's guy in LA became curious about Spencer after watching Hannibal Newton's report on the discovery of remains at the ranch in Wyoming. In one of the follow-up news reports, it had been mentioned that Spencer Christmas hoped to find his own mother's remains among the dead. The lab technician realized Spencer's DNA must've been run and was now part of the universal database, so he checked the results and then compared them to his own. The discrepancies regarding the mitochondrial matches worried him so he checked all the siblings' DNA found in the database and then compared them to his own reports. He saw the same discrepancies. Jasper knew Nestor was Spencer's primary investigator for the ranch-house-discovery ordeal, so before Jasper and his family boarded a flight to Phoenix, Holly emailed him the accurate DNA reports. They would hear from Nestor after his results were compared to those identified and unidentified remains.

It fell silent at the table, heavy. Then, almost like Nobel Prize-winning poetry, Spencer's cellphone beeped and so did Jasper's. The brothers scowled at the faces of their cellphones and then at each other.

"The results are in," Holly said, sweeping into the dining room like a lovely but mighty wind. She plopped in the seat beside her husband, keeping her curious gaze trained on Spencer. "This is good news though, right?"

Spencer slowly turned to look at me. His lips were slightly parted until he closed his mouth to swallow and then say, "My mother's alive."

CHAPTER TWELVE

JADA FORTE

S pencer's mother's birth name was Charlotte Wright, and she currently resided in Philadelphia, Pennsylvania. Nestor's DNA specialist was able to track her through second cousins and sibling matches. The relief was that she wasn't one of the dead women. The setback was Charlotte wasn't living by her real name, which obviously meant she didn't want to be found. But the clincher was she was living by the name of Danielle Spencer. We all concluded that the fact she had chosen Spencer as her phony last name had to have been deliberate.

Jasper then shared his experience about connecting with his late mother's relatives. Spencer listened quietly. I tried to read his expression, but he was playing poker face again, which meant the only way to know what he was feeling or thinking would be to ask him. I settled on doing so when we were alone later in the day. However, I got the feeling he hadn't truly expected his mother to be alive.

Before I could reach over and take Spencer's hand to let him know I would be by his side no matter how he decided to handle the issue of his birth mother, he clapped his hands together and said, "Let's deal with one shitshow at a time. Irina, Charlotte, or any other woman associated with Randolph and Valentine aren't going to feel safe until Valentine is taken care of." Spencer glared at his watch. "We should get down to the lab and take a look at those videos."

Jasper was nodding continuously. "We have to make some calls too, finish cutting all of Valentine's lifelines. The difficulty won't be getting him arrested. It will be keeping him in prison."

Spencer agreed and then finally turned to look at me. He couldn't hold eye contact with me while he said the three of them were driving to the evidence processing lab and he wondered if I minded remaining behind.

I gulped, wanting so fervently to kiss him deeply as I gently put two fingers under his chin to garner deep and intense eye contact between us. I got it loud and clear. Irina, Valentine, the dead girls in the wall, and the fake DNA profiles of the Christmas siblings, it was all bigger than me and preceded me. I didn't need to be so involved. Plus, Jasper and Holly seemed to be a formidable duo. Spencer was in good hands.

"It's fine," I said.

Finally, our lips merged and our tongues brushed tenderly. My head spun.

"I love you," I whispered unthinkingly.

Spencer's lips played with a smile. "I love you too."

Holly drummed excitedly on the table. "All right then. Let's go nail Valentine's ass to the wall."

She and Jasper gazed at each other. They were communicating without words and were definitely on the same page. There was something about Holly that made me feel so damn inadequate. I didn't like carrying that feeling and was happy when they all finally left so I could figure out how to deal with what was going on inside me.

───────

SPENCER HADN'T TOUCHED HIS BREAKFAST, AND I

hoped that at some point during the day he'd eat something. He had a way of missing meals when he was stressed, and when he did, he was extra crabby.

I forced myself to finish eating, and when my belly was full, I went back to our room to retrieve my phone. I asked Lourdes if there were more permeable women's clothes anywhere on the property, and she brought me a sundress with flip-flops. When I asked where she got them, she said over the years many women had left articles of clothing behind and she kept them in a closet for times such as this.

"You're all the same size," she said.

I chuckled because I knew it wasn't a compliment. However, I always could appreciate a well-placed, carefully constructed insult.

Now that I was wearing less wintery clothes, my phone and I went for a walk under the trees. I had so many text and voice messages that my mailbox was full, and my phone had even stopped accepting texts. I never forgot what Spencer had said in the car in Toronto though. Hope had been trying to contact me. The fact that I kept my phone in airplane mode even when I wasn't on an airplane had always driven her crazy.

She was the first person I called, and as usual

when she was eager to hear from me, she picked up on the first ring.

"What the fuck!" she yelled.

I tossed my head back and laughed. "Sorry!"

"Don't sorry me. If Perry and Spencer didn't know each other, I wouldn't know if you were fucking dead or alive or being held captive by your crazy-ass mother."

I gasped and flopped onto the nearest iron bench. "Oh my God, Hope, you know she tried to imprison me?"

"Well, duh," she said, not sounding even a tiny bit surprised. "She's fucking crazy. Now do you believe me?"

I let out a long sigh, melting against the bench. "I do. Unfortunately, I do."

"So what the hell happened to you?" Hope asked.

I started from the moment I had walked into my mother's hospital room and ended with Spencer and I making an escape and flying to Toronto.

"What were you doing in Toronto?" she asked.

I felt the corners of my mouth turn downward. "I can't tell you." I sounded so sad, and I was because I hated not being able to divulge everything about my recent escapades to Hope. Not only did I have to keep what I had found in my mother's closet a secret but also everything I knew about Irina and Spencer's birth mom.

"That Spencer Christmas is a secretive one, isn't he?" she asked.

I turned my head slightly. "Did Perry tell you that?"

She chuckled. "Yes, he did. He said Spencer had always done more listening than speaking, and he never divulged anything more than what everyone already knew about him."

I snickered. "That's true. I'm finally getting him to open up. Oh," I said with a stop, suddenly remembering. "He asked me to marry him while we were fucking."

Hope let out a laugh so loud that I had to pull the phone away from my ear.

"But," I said, once she had simmered down. "He clarified that he meant it once his dick was out of me."

"My goodness, are you guys doing a lot of fucking?" Hope asked.

I rolled my eyes exaggeratedly. "We can't keep our hands off each other."

"Jeez, my little virgin friend has discovered fucking, and now there's no stopping her."

I cupped the phone closer to my ear and then searched up and down the path. No one was coming. "Right," I said, easily dismissing her sarcasm. "But I wanted to ask you something."

"You're whispering, so it must be a sex question."

"Yes," I said, still whispering.

"Shoot, and no pun intended."

I rolled my eyes sarcastically. "I remember you and Ling and the others say you fake orgasms and only have real ones if a guy is going down on you, but Spencer makes me feel the same sensation, well, most of the time, when his penis is inside me. Is that normal?"

I waited for Hope's answer, but she remained so quiet I thought our call had dropped.

"Hope?" I asked, checking to see if she was still there.

"Jada?" she finally said.

I frowned, detecting the seriousness in her tone. "Yes."

"Word of advice."

"Okay?" I sang curiously.

"Don't ever fucking tell another woman that. Keep Spencer's dick of gold to yourself. Like, verbally and literally."

I was waiting for her to laugh, but she didn't. She followed up by confirming it was not normal and Spencer simply knew his way around a pussy.

"But I'm not marrying Perry for his sexual powers, which leads me to why I've been trying to reach you ever since you hung up in my face—and I forgive you for that."

I sniffed a chuckle. "Thank you, I'm sorry. You were right."

"No need to grovel," I pictured her rolling her eyes when she said that. "I still love you, and that's why on Saturday, I need you to play the role of my maid of honor."

"You're getting married this weekend?" I asked, sounding distracted because I was. A question had landed in my head that had nothing to do with her wedding.

"Yes. In Hawaii. At Perry's family mansion on the Kona coast. You and Spencer are cordially invited. For your main course, would you like the steak, glazed duck, rock lobster, or all three?" Her tone sounded lackluster, and it concerned me.

My shoulders dropped and curled. "I'll have the rock lobster, but I'm not sure if Spencer can make it. He has a lot going on. But I—"

"Wait, I just looked at my calendar. The

wedding is not this Saturday. It's the following Saturday."

I sighed as I rolled my eyes. I never heard someone be so willy-nilly about a wedding, and I sure as hell didn't expect such behavior from her.

"Are you sure you want to do this, get married?" I asked, shaking my head softly.

Hope paused. "I want to be Perry's wife more than anything I've ever wanted in my life," she fervently declared.

"But it's not like you to forget the date of your wedding. You're the sort of person who remembers details down to the font you would choose for the napkins. So why the blasé attitude?"

An insect buzzed by my ear, and I swatted after it.

"You know me so well," she said with a tired sigh. "That's one of many reasons why I love you."

She went on to tell me how Perry's mother, whom she referred to as Old Money Mama, caught wind that they had planned to elope. She showed up at their doorstep and guilt-tripped Perry into changing his mind.

"Barbara and Patricia could swap recipes for the fine art of mind-fucking their children. Anyway, Barbara planned it all, not me. All I'm supposed to do is show up. All the bridesmaids are Perry's cousins or something. However, I told her that the maid of honor is mine. She belongs to me."

"Shit," I said as another fly zoomed past my ear.

"Is everything okay?" Hope asked.

"It was a fly, I think. Sometimes I forget how much of a city girl I am." I sprang to my feet and started back toward the house. I'd rather swim than sit under an insect-attracting tree anyway. "But it isn't so easy when you have your own Patricia Forte to deal with, is it?" I asked, getting back on subject.

"What?" she snapped, sounding confused.

"You're always advising me to defy my mom's controlling ways, and here you are letting Barbara tell you when, where, and how to get married. The Hope Calloway I know would tell Old Money Mama to fuck off."

She hummed inquisitively. "You're fucking right. My goodness."

I pictured her incessantly shaking her head as she often did when she was riled up about something.

"Okay well, stay tuned for another Perry and Hope nuptials update," she announced.

I would've asked her to share some highlights of

what was to come, but that question I'd had before she told me about her future-mother-in-law-sponsored wedding was still knocking around in my head.

"Hope, could I ask you something?"

Her grunt was laced by intrigue. "Sounds serious."

Suddenly I stopped in my tracks. "You've known me for a long time, so I want to know what you think about who I've become."

"Who you've become?"

I started walking again. "Yes. How do you see me?"

"You're gonna have to provide a theme here," she said.

I decided to not go through the front door and put up with all the hoopla of the staff asking if I wanted this, that, or the other. Plus, Jane was still in the house, and for some reason, I was too nervous to run into her. So I headed up a cobblestone path flanked on both sides by white rock beds. As the route rounded the side of the house, I recalled how Spencer had just appeared on our patio yesterday. I was attempting to find the same entrance.

"A theme?" I asked.

"Yes, are we talking about your parental relationship, love life…"

I tilted my head back and said, "Ah, now I got it. It's career."

She grunted thoughtfully. "Why are you asking?"

My mind flashed back to breakfast this morning, how Holly was so much a part of what was going on in Spencer's and her husband's lives, while caring for Jane who was sitting on her lap. She was the picture of perfection as far as I was concerned. Suddenly, I knew that was why I didn't want to run into toddler Jane. She belonged to Holly's perfect life, and I felt as if I didn't have the right to intrude.

"I met Holly Christmas," I whispered, not wanting anyone to hear me.

"Ah, I see… You're comparing yourself to her."

I felt a small sense of victory when I saw the balcony to our room. "I guess so." It felt therapeutic to admit that to Hope.

"Don't do that. Just be yourself, Jada. Who you are is good enough. It's better than good enough. You're perfect. As far as career, sure you've been trying to figure it out, but I think the reason you haven't fully committed to what you love is because it's so connected to your mother. And you're always fucking sprinting in the opposite direction of her until she figures out how to catch you."

I walked across the patio and sat on the edge of the swimming pool and let my feet dangle in the water.

"I don't get it," I said, although deep down I sort of did.

"Whenever I used to go to your place and the TV was on, you'd be watching something that had to do with the world of politics. You'd give me a breakdown of what was happening under the surface. You knew a lot of those people and who they were associated with, which was why you were able to tell me why they were making a particular argument."

My eyebrows pulled so tight that my temples ached. "So you're saying I should be a political commentator? Because I don't like those slimy assholes either."

"I didn't say you should be one of them, but it's always been obvious to me that you know politics on a level that most of us do not, and you seem to like it more than the rest of us. You don't let it get you all twisted and turned. You listen to it in a pragmatic way."

It fell silent between us, and I was sure Hope

was happy about that. She had skillfully used lawyering to bring her case for my future to my ears, and now it was time for me to deliberate.

There was something I'd been trying to not accept for quite a while. I'd had fun working on Jimmy's campaign even though I despised him. I was good at influencing public perception of one of the biggest dicks I'd ever had the displeasure of meeting. I laughed when Alice had suggested Spencer run for Congress, but the more I thought about it, the more I saw how, despite his father's reputation, he was a hundred times more electable than Jimmy. People loved a comeback story, and they really went crazy for the one who had atonement as their major plot point. Spencer could win. I knew it.

"Listen, Jada, I have to go but keep your goddamn phone off airplane mode unless you're—"

"On an airplane," I finished for her.

"I sound like a broken record because you keep doing it."

I sighed hard, thinking about why I was so used to putting my device in avoidant mode. "I'll keep it out of airplane," I said, figuring the time had come for me to apply less drastic tactics in efforts to avoid my mom. I'd noticed she had called and left several voice messages recently. The woman had no shame apparently. The thought of whatever she could have to say to me sent shivers down my spine.

"We'll see," Hope said. I pictured her rolling her eyes.

We said goodbye to each other and ended our call. The first thing I did was delete my mother's messages and block her number from calling my device. I'd done that many times before and she had always found a way to reach me. Then, my phone rang in my hand. I raised my eyebrows as I leaned back, reading the name Jimmy Douchebag on the screen.

"What the…" I whispered, pondering whether I should let my voicemail tell him my mailbox was too full. On a split-second decision, I hit the Answer button.

"What do you want, Jimmy?" I asked.

He scoffed. "You sound as if you hate me or something."

I squished one side of my face as I shrugged. "Well, yeah, I kind of do. What do you want?"

"Ouch, Jada," he said emphatically. "That fucking hurts because I like you."

I rolled my eyes hard. "What do you want, Jimmy?" I asked, enunciating each syllable clearly.

"I want to talk to you about your mother."

"My interests are no longer aligned with her politically, so—"

"I promise you, you want to hear this."

"Okay," I said, shaking my head and shrugging. "What is it?"

"I can't tell you on the phone."

I sighed forcefully. "Goodbye, Jimmy."

"No. Wait a minute, Jada. Fuck, I'm being nice to you and you're treating me like shit."

I twisted my mouth thoughtfully. He was right. Shit. "Listen, I can't meet with you right now because I'm in Phoenix, and—"

"You're there with Christmas guy?" Jimmy asked with an edge.

I furrowed my eyebrows and then released them. "Yes. You know his name, so it's rude of you to refer to him as 'Christmas guy.' And how do you know I'm with Spencer after telling you I'm in Phoenix?"

"It's all over the news, what he found in the storage unit. But how are you involved?" he asked.

"I'm sorry?"

"What does Spencer finding shit about his

father's crimes in a storage unit have to do with you?"

"Nothing," I said, sounding defensive.

"So is that why you quit my campaign, to follow Christmas around the fucking country? Because that's what guys like him are into. His pussy in his bed whenever his dick wants it."

"What?" I snapped, seeing red, angry about how he minimized my connection with Spencer to fucking sexualized body parts. "That was fucking vulgar. And you know what, I still don't know exactly why you're on my phone. You have five seconds to convince me to not hang up," I roared, shaking with anger and disappointed because I let the little twat get to me.

He laughed, knowing he was effective. I had the mind to hang up on him, but I was too curious about what he wanted to say about my mother to do it at the moment.

"One. Two. Three——"

"Wait, Jada. Sure, you've seen me behave like an arrogant prick. I'm working on that as we speak. And…" He sighed. "I don't want you to hate me." He actually sounded sincere, but I knew his tone was meant to influence me. Jimmy was a true narcissist. He could give a damn if I or anyone else hated him. All he wanted was to extract from us what he wanted and would do or say anything to get it.

I forced a hard breath out of my nostrils. "As I said, I'm not in California or DC, so whatever you want to tell me about my mother in person will have to wait."

"Christmas. Phoenix," he said as if he were reading off a short list.

"What?" I asked, snarling.

"I'll see you soon."

I shook my head like a rattle. "What?"

Our call had ended. When I called him again, the line kept ringing. The third time I tried to reach him, I was sent straight to voicemail.

I sighed forcefully and set my phone on the concrete beside me. What the fuck was Jimmy planning on doing? Something told me he was going to show up on the doorstep of the mansion.

"No way," I whispered.

Then I visualized Spencer being so angry to see him that he punched Jimmy, who was a mere mouse next to Spencer, dead in his face.

"Hello, miss," a woman said hesitantly.

I quickly whipped my face around to see a girl about my age walking a happy toddler toward me.

She had come through an entrance on the opposite side of the patio I had entered.

Little Jane tore toward the pool as if it were the best thing since sliced bread. I quickly pulled my legs out of the water and got to my feet.

"How can I help you?" My heart beat nervously.

The young woman stopped but Jane kept trying to walk, twisting and turning and giggling as she couldn't wait to dive headfirst into the water. "I'm September, Jane's nanny. Our pool is cold, and Lourdes said it will take an hour before it heats but that yours is already warm. Do you mind if we join you?" She beamed down at Jane. "She can't wait another minute."

It was as if Jane knew exactly what her nanny had asked of me because she lifted her little rosy cheeks into the cutest smile and began making noises as if she were emphatically trying to convince me to say yes.

I felt my smile grow as big as the sun as I enthusiastically said, "Of course!"

We all got into the swimming pool together. Soon Lourdes had someone bring us loads of pool toys for Jane, and that was the beginning of my jolly good time with Holly and Jasper's daughter.

CHAPTER THIRTEEN

SPENCER CHRISTMAS

"What the fuck," Jasper whispered with his eyes narrowed, watching the repulsive shit occurring on the screen.

I kept recoiling too, wanting to run the fuck away from what I was seeing. It was sick, strange, and seemed unreal in the way that it was the sort of shit that happened in a B-movie, meant to shock more than entertain.

The videotapes were old but in pristine condition from being kept in an air-conditioned storage unit for so many years. There was no doubt the old bastard with a girl who was old enough to be his fucking great-granddaughter was Arthur Valentine. He kept rubbing her as if he was putting lotion on her skin. The girl had the same death and darkness in her eyes as the one whom my father had been dragging through the hallway years ago. However, Valentine was wearing a diaper and an adult-sized baby T-shirt. He was kicking his legs and pounding the floor, throwing a tantrum as if he were an infant.

"Is this shit for real?" Jasper asked, as the girl, who had no tits at all, would put her chest against his mouth and he would go eerily still and quiet as he sucked.

"That's the most disturbing thing I've ever seen," Holly muttered, glaring at the video.

"I'm…" I shook my head. I was fucking flabbergasted, fucking floored.

"Turn it off, Joe," Agent Ben Martinez said.

The technician working the video system followed Martinez's order.

"There's a lot of the same sort of capture on the other videotapes," Martinez said.

No matter what I tried, I couldn't get what I just saw out of my head. I had to force myself to stop harping on it. "Was her name provided by Irina?"

"Yes," Martinez said, nodding. "I never had such detailed evidence fall into our lap this way.

We've already located three of the girls, who are now much older of course."

"What about Valentine?" Jasper asked.

"We picked him up two hours ago," Martinez replied.

Jasper and I looked at each other. On the ride to the station, Holly drove while he and I made calls to Valentine's usual allies, warning them to not pull strings to get the old man out on bond or else. He was to sit in jail until he was tried, convicted, and sentenced to life in prison.

"And Irina, what about her?" I asked.

Martinez folded his skinny arms. "Phase two."

"Phase two?" I asked, wondering if that was supposed to mean something to me.

Martinez's hand came down on my shoulder. "I need you to come with me."

I felt my forehead collapse into a frown and my jaw pull tight. The way he'd said that worried the hell out of me. When I looked at Jasper to see if he knew why Martinez was separating us, he shook his head.

"What's going on, Ben?" Holly asked, her expression eager as hell.

Martinez smirked. "Holly, don't push."

"Don't push? What the hell, Ben?"

Martinez raised his hand to gesture but froze as he was about to say something. Suddenly, he sighed. "I'm pretty sure your husband is going to handle the details you need to run with your story before the other vultures get it."

She narrowed an eye. "That depends on how tight your seams are."

He smirked at her, appearing as if he was both annoyed and impressed by her. "We have no leakers here."

She shrugged. "We'll see."

"I know."

"All right," Jasper barked, sounding irritated by the back and forth between his wife and the FBI agent.

Jasper was a jealous kind of guy, and perhaps I was too. I tried to picture Jada standing here bantering back and forth with a good-looking guy like Martinez. *Yeah*, I wouldn't like it either.

"Okay," I said an octave louder than my usual voice. "Show me what you got, Martinez." I turned toward Holly. "Whatever I learn, you'll be the first to know."

She pointed at me. "I'm counting on it, Spencer."

My gaze shifted to Jasper, who nodded approvingly.

EVERY HALLWAY WITH HIGH-GLOSSED WAXED FLOORS scuffed up by the enormous amount of foot traffic smelled the same. I couldn't pinpoint the scent, but a cleaning solution and male body odor was involved.

"So where are you taking me?" I asked Martinez, following him down the hall.

The man walked upright like all law enforcement officers did, standing tall and confident even though his frame was short and slight.

"There's someone who wants to meet you."

I'd been grimacing so much lately that my temples ached when I didn't. "Who?"

He turned to glance at me. "I'd rather show you." He stopped in front of a door, which had Q1 on it, and opened it.

I waited to walk in after him, but he stood there and kept holding the door open.

I dipped my head to the side. "All right, sure," I said as I walked into the room.

I saw a table with two chairs, one on each side of it. One chair was empty, and the other was occupied by a woman in a police officer's uniform. She and I connected eyes for a second. She seemed awed by the sight of me and then abruptly she rose to her feet.

"You're Spencer," she said, sounding breathless.

Again, my eyebrows were pulling too tight, giving me a fucking headache. I needed for all this shit to be over sooner rather than later so I could make love to my woman and sleep for days on end.

"I am," I said.

Her face began to twitch as if she were fighting to hold her sober expression.

"Good luck, Captain," Martinez said.

I turned in time to see him close the door. When I faced her again, she pointed her hand at the chair nearest me.

"Could you please sit?"

I leaned away from her. "Is everything okay? Nothing happened to Irina Petrov, did it?"

"Irina Petrov is safe," she said.

I tilted my head. I hadn't expected her to reply as if she knew whom I was talking about. "Then you know it was her who led me to the storage unit with all the evidence."

Her solemn expression remained unchanged.

The longer I looked at the officer, the more I noticed. Her face was red, eyes watery. She had a tough exterior that couldn't hide her natural beauty. Now she was looking at me as if she were pleading for me to sit so she could get the show on the road. Without prolonging it any further, I did what she had asked.

Slowly, cautiously, she sat too.

First, she stared at me, and the longer our gazes remained posted on each other, the more familiar she started to look.

"Do I know you?" I asked.

"I know Irina," she said.

"Okay…" I wanted to massage my temples. Shit, my headache was becoming unbearable.

"It's no mistake the storage unit is located in Phoenix. It's because I'm here."

I tilted my head curiously, not too mentally exhausted to leave the pieces unplaced. "Did she come to you after she somehow escaped the ranch?"

The woman swallowed as her frown intensified. "I knew her before she escaped the ranch."

I leaned so far back in my chair that I had to stop myself from toppling over "Who are you?" My voice came out in a whisper.

She cleared her throat. "I want to tell you a story about a girl who was twelve years old."

My lips were fastened together too tightly to speak. All I could do was nod.

She started by telling me the girl was a runaway from Portland, Maine. Her mother was a narcissist, who couldn't live without a man warming her bed. The girl's biological father was a drunk and thief, who spent more of his life in jail than out. Her mother's first boyfriend had beat her mother and the girl too. He hated females but loved to hurt them. If it weren't for the same police officer who got the call to come to the house whenever a neighbor reported abuse, the mother probably would've kept the man around until he killed both of them one day. However, an officer named Sam Schwartz had threatened the guy, and the man had been smart enough to understand Schwartz's threat wasn't empty.

After that guy left, the girl's mother went to the bar and picked up another loser. This one liked girls a lot, so much so that after the mother passed out from too much vodka, the man would crawl into bed with the girl and do things to her that she thought were never possible. Then her mother married that man, but the man never stopped. One day, the mother, in a drunken haze, caught the man on top of the girl, and instead of putting the man out, she threw her twelve-year-old daughter out of the house.

For days and nights the girl roamed the streets, sleeping in alleys, eating out of trash cans, scared, alone and wanting to go back home. On the night she had decided to go back home and beg her mother to forgive her for whatever she had done to make her stepfather touch her and hurt her in such a way, she met another girl her age who convinced her she could get food, a comfortable bed, and safety if she just followed her.

That girl took her to a big house with lots of other girls. There were beds, good meals, and a loving house mother who'd said she understood the depth of the girl's pain. She said the girl's real mother was a selfish bitch who would never keep her safe, which was true. The woman said she would be a better mother. In that house, the girl would receive love in all forms.

At first, they would drug the girl's food and drink. At night, in her dreams, a man wearing a black hood and black smock would come to her room, spread her legs, and force himself inside her. In the morning, she would feel what had happened to her but still didn't know if it had been real or not.

"Then one day, the girl's belly began to grow. The house mother told her she was going on a trip to a bigger house, a place with horses and cows. She would be happy there," the officer said.

By now I was on the edge of my seat. I had already figured out the girl was her. My chest was tight because I also suspected who the girl, the woman, and police officer might be. Only, Nestor's intel had said my mother lived in Philadelphia. Nestor had never gotten his information wrong, never.

"How did you escape?" I asked before realizing what had come out of my mouth.

The officer stared into my eyes for a long moment. My gaze lowered to her trembling hands, and when she saw I was looking at them, she abruptly put them under the table.

"I gave birth at that ranch. And at that ranch, I saw girls being abused by men every day. They could do whatever the hell they wanted to us back then." She sniffed and then rubbed under her nose before sitting up straighter. "You came early." She narrowed her eyes at me, and I assumed she was examining my reaction.

I wanted to scrub my hands over my face and squeeze my eyes shut, hoping that when I removed my hands and opened my eyes, I would've disappeared from this room, this moment, and from the sight of this woman, who no doubt was my mother.

When I looked at her again, her expression hadn't changed. She was giving me a moment to process, but it was clear she wasn't done with her story.

"They dropped me off at the local hospital. I had no ID, and I was too afraid to tell them where I came from. I lost a lot of blood giving birth to you. I knew I had you after experiencing the most vile kind of abuse, but you were mine," she said, her chin trembling. "I planned to have you and escape and go anywhere safe where no one could touch us.

"In the middle of the night, weak and blood pressure through the roof, I hobbled to the nursery, and when I got there, you were already gone. Then I heard a nurse say that the girl in my room was missing and they needed to find her because they had found her mother. I knew they were coming to take me back to that ranch, and I wasn't going."

The police officer's tough exterior no longer existed. I had become immobilized. I was in her story. I was the fucking baby missing in the nursery.

She wanted to collect me and run away. I felt glad she hadn't succeeded, and that spooked the shit out of me.

The officer took a deep breath through her nose as she pulled herself together again.

"I made it to the parking lot," she said.

"What's your name?" I asked out of the blue. I realized she'd been talking to me for a while, and I'd never got her name.

She shifted abruptly and then looked from one corner of the room to the next. "My real name is Charlotte Wright," she whispered. "But I go by Danielle Spencer."

Nestor had that part right.

"Why Danielle Spencer?" I asked.

She narrowed her eyes and smashed her lips together.

"I do that a lot," I said.

Her eyes narrowed. "You do what a lot?"

I pointed at her face. "That expression you're showing me. I got it from you, I guess."

She sniffed and so did I.

I shrugged and took a deep breath. "So you're my mother?"

"I am. And I've known all about you. Followed you throughout the years. I hoped to hell those men didn't fuck you up. They were sick, both of them. I would've loved to put the both of them behind bars, but Valentine and Christmas were more powerful than I'd ever be. They owned police departments, judges, members of Congress and depending on who was sitting in the top seat, the president."

That was it. That was why I'd rather have grown in the misery of being Randolph Christmas's son. I had lived through hell, but now I was powerful enough to make one of those men pay for what he had done to my mother and countless other girls. But I had more questions.

"Irina escaped the night all the girls were killed. Her leg was found in the wall. How did that happen?" I asked.

The woman who was my mother continued the tale of her past. That night, Irina found her in the parking lot. She had begged Irina to not take her back. She fell to her knees crying, promising to never tell anyone, not say a word.

"Something clicked in Irina that night, I think. She was dutiful to Randolph, who told her what to do with the girls from New York or Rhode Island. For the longest time, I thought she was scared of him, but later I learned she had always hated him and had planned to one day, when the time was right and she knew he couldn't buy himself out of a conviction, turn him in for kidnapping, child abuse, abduction, and rape, among other crimes like sex trafficking, both domestic and international."

"Then we have solid proof?" I asked. At that moment, I was unable to see the woman as my mother. In my eyes, she was the key to putting Valentine away.

"Valentine wasn't associated with the ranch," she said. "However, he trusted Irina to do work for him until one day he found out that she'd been recording his sick escapades with underage girls. That's why he wanted her dead, along with the girls in the house."

Struck by illumination, I leaned forward abruptly in my chair. "Are you telling me the girls in the videos with Valentine are the ones who are in the wall?"

"He dumped them at the ranch after using them. He never intended for those girls to live to adulthood," Charlotte said. She scratched the side of her face thoughtfully. "The night Irina found me in the parking lot, she said she was tired of what was happening at the ranch, and we drove back to get all the girls and get the hell out of there. She had money, lots of it, all she had stolen from Valentine and Randolph. We were all going to disappear until we were old enough to tell our stories.

"But when we had gotten back to the ranch, it was a bloodbath. A mute named Gordon, the muscle around the ranch, used to restrain the girls whenever one of us broke into a fit, wanting to run away or just go into a rage. He had killed them all with a chainsaw. Anyway, it had been my job to get the keys to the bus that was in the north side garage. The keys were hanging on a placard in the hallway between the entrance of the main house and the garage. Getting them was a piece of cake because there was no one on that side of the house, not even Mother.

"I got the keys and went into the north side garage and waited in the van for what felt like an eternity. I got worried, so I opened the garage door and drove to the front of the house. The lights were off throughout most the house, and I thought to myself: the lights were never off in those parts. I contemplated driving off to save my own life, but instead I went to the area of the house where the lights were on, and before I got there, I heard Irina screaming. It was a sound that still haunts me today.

"Gordon was holding a chainsaw and had sliced her leg off. I felt as though I left my body in that moment—saw the blood and him laughing, covered in blood as body parts of girls were strewn on the floor around. He had gone mad with violence. I needed to save her. So I saw a machete on the ground next to a girl named Carolina's head. I knew I'd probably get one chance to strike him. If I missed, he'd kill me and Irina as he'd done the others, but I had to do something. He was on the verge of sawing off Irina's other leg when I whipped the machete through the air, and somehow the blade went straight through his neck, decapitating him."

"Shit," I whispered, rubbing the skin above my lip. Charlotte's recount of the night had been so vivid that I could picture her as a small girl, thirteen by then but strong enough to slice a man's head off.

"He must've sharpened the blade," she said, perhaps answering the thoughts in my head that she could likely read on my face.

She told me she drove Irina to the hospital, and on the way, while Irina was lucid, she told Charlotte to go back to the ranch, finish chopping up Gordon, and put the machete and chainsaw in the van and then dig a hole and bury Gordon's body parts.

I jerked my head backward. "Let me get this right. Thirteen years old, you went back to the ranch, sliced a grown man to pieces and then buried him?"

She sighed dejectedly. "I did."

I thought about my search team combing every inch of that compound. "Did you bury him on the property?"

"No," she said, shaking her head assuredly. "Irina instructed me to do it off the property. She wanted it to look as if he purposely disappeared after the murders. A few years later, she contacted Randolph as Gordon, and he paid her for the job."

I felt my nose wrinkling. "You mean the job of killing the girls?"

She nodded and muttered, "Yes."

I took a deep breath to steady myself. This was shocking shit I was listening to. It almost seemed unreal, but it was definitely real.

"Where did you bury him?" I asked.

"I don't know exactly, but I gave the FBI the general location. They're searching. How did you know to search for the bodies?" she asked.

I told her about overhearing my father and Arthur Valentine. "Their conversation had haunted me for a long time. Then one day, I decided to look. And not only search but think like my father would to find the bodies."

Charlotte tilted her head, examining me. "You've gone pale. I've said a lot, probably too much in one sitting. Do you need a break?"

She looked concerned about me in a way that no woman besides Jada ever had.

"I don't need a break," I whispered past the tightness in my throat. "You're not being charged for the murder of this Gordon guy, are you?"

She shook her head. "No, I'm not. The evidence proves he was a mass murderer and I had to stop him from killing Irina. Plus, I was a thirteen-year-old girl who had been terrorized and abused."

I sighed with relief, although I knew she wasn't going to be charged, but I needed to ask. "That's good to hear."

It fell silent between us. I couldn't take my eyes off her face.

"You're actually my mother," I whispered.

"I—" She hesitated and then cleared her throat. "I am."

We stared at each other. As each second passed, I became less dizzy, and that sick feeling in the pit of my stomach began to resolve itself.

"And you're a cop?" I asked.

She pressed her lips and nodded, becoming

extra emotional when I asked that. "Twenty-three years."

Shit, a wall of something that felt damn good struck me. What was it? It could've been pride. "You went through what you experienced, and you became a law enforcement officer?"

Her smile broadened. "I'm a captain."

I shook my head slowly. "How?"

"When I left Wyoming, I was weak, sick, and I only knew one person to call for help, Sam."

I raised a finger pointedly, recalling the name she had mentioned earlier. "Sam Schwartz, the officer who threatened your mother's abusive boyfriend?"

Her smile was nothing but pure joy now. "He and Gladys, his wife, took me in."

"Are they still alive?" I asked in a rush.

She sat up straighter. "Yeah," she whispered, nodding.

"Is he the reason you're a cop?"

"Yeah," she replied still choked up.

We stared at each other. That shameful thing I had felt earlier, as if I were better off with the Christmas's billions, had dissipated. Law enforcement would've been my legacy if my mother could've found a way to take me before Randolph's people had gotten their paws on me. I would've been a great cop.

"You see…" I coughed to clear my throat. I needed to gather my thoughts and let her know exactly what was on my mind.

"You don't have to—"

"No." I shook my head emphatically. "I want to say this. Because you see, I'm looking at this beautiful woman and strong woman who survived what Randolph had done to her. You made it out of the darkness."

"It wasn't easy," she muttered.

I nodded understandingly. "Shedding demons never is. I had my own."

Suddenly, she reached across the table to put her hands on mine. "I'm sorry to have left you with him. I built my career on one day being strong enough to confront him." She flopped back in her chair and let her head fall back. "Then he died." When she glared at me again, the vengeance in her eyes was recognizable.

A knock on the door made us both jump. When the door opened, Martinez poked his head in.

"Petrov's here, and she's asking for the both of you," he said.

"We'll be there in a second," Charlotte said,

sounding secure and having a natural voice of authority.

Martinez narrowed his eyes at both of our faces, nodded once, and carefully closed the door.

Now that we were alone again, my mother and I continued staring silently at each other. The sense of euphoria that was parked inside me felt unreal. I was also confused about our next step, and I was sure she was too.

"Now what?" I asked.

She shrugged. "I don't know. I've dreamed of this moment, and now, I don't know what to do."

"How about we meet again soon and talk some more?" I asked.

I noticed her hands trembling, and more than that, she didn't try to hide them.

She sniffed as tears rolled freely down her face. "I'd like that."

We stood at the same time. I watched her approach me like a deer in headlights. When the woman whom I thought I'd never lay eyes on hugged me, my mind went blank, and my body rigid. But she kept clinging to me, never letting go. Slowly, something inside me began to melt. I didn't know what the fuck was happening to me. It was the way she smelled, like flowers and desert wind.

Her body was thin but strong. I brushed the side of my face against the top of her head. All of what I was feeling must've been how I experienced her in the womb. And I must've gotten lost in a daze because only now had I noticed she was shaking like a leaf while weeping.

I LET MY MOTHER CLING TO ME AS LONG AS SHE needed. The minutes passed, and she recovered slowly. When she finally let me go, I kissed her forehead and said, "I'm not going anywhere, Mother." It wasn't difficult for me to call her that, even though it felt strange.

Choked up and with her chin still slightly quivering, she nodded.

I gave her a moment to wipe her face and then she laughed and said. "So fucking emotional here."

I chuckled. "It's emotional for me too."

She rubbed her stomach. "The last I was this close to you, you were here. Now look at you. And you found those bodies." She beamed at me. "That was a proud moment for me."

This time, I threw my arms around her. She reciprocated. Then I walked to the door and held it open for her to pass. She gently patted the side of my face, smiling tightly on her way out. I followed behind her and watched her walk, standing tall and strong like all the other law enforcement officers in the building.

CHAPTER FOURTEEN

JADA FORTE

I was sound asleep when I heard Spencer softly calling my name. Gradually, I found my way to consciousness. When my eyes opened, he was lying beside me, grinning from ear to ear.

"Hey," I whispered. "You look happy."

His neck craned downward and our lips, then tongues, melted. "Babe, I met my mother."

I felt my eyelids expand, and suddenly, I was fully awake. "No shit? How?"

"I'll tell you all about it, but first…" Spencer guided me onto my back and parted my thighs.

I sighed as he inserted his rigid cock inside me.

"I missed you, baby," he whispered, his eyes closed as he indulged in my wetness.

With my arms wrapped around him tightly, I confessed that I missed him more.

AT SOME POINT, SPENCER GUIDED ME ONTO MY SIDE to enter my pussy from the rear. He loved being inside me that way. It always brought him to orgasm faster, and this time was no different. After we both allowed our bodies to calm down, he began to tell me about his meeting with his mother.

I listened attentively while he revealed that she was a police officer and what she had gone through days after giving birth to him. By the time he'd gotten to the videos of Valentine costumed like an infant and performing strange sexual acts on young girls, his cock had gone all the way down and we were facing each other.

"The videos have already been leaked to BCN."

I grinned. "You mean you leaked them?"

He winked at me. "So people will know exactly why he was arrested."

The flirtatious and genial moment between us was short-lived. It had to be after all he had just said to me.

"So Holly did the interviews at the station?"

"Yes, she did," he said, regarding me curiously. "How do you feel about her?"

My posture suddenly became rigid. "Why do you ask?"

"I noticed you were uncomfortable at breakfast."

I closed my eyes and let my head fall back. "Oh, I see." When I looked at his sexy face again, he was watching me expectantly. "Not much gets past you, does it?"

His expression remained serious. "I want to know how you felt."

I twisted my mouth, embarrassed about telling the truth. However, if there was anyone to be honest with, it was Spencer. He had proven I could trust him a million times over. "Jealous," I blurted.

"You don't have to be."

I sighed. "I know you love me, but I felt you had a residual crush on her. I mean, look at her. She's..." I shook my head trying to come up with the appropriate adjective.

"She's not you," he said. "And you're not her. When I first met Holly, I was a different person. When my brother showed interest in her, I pursued her in the way I used to pursue women back then, only because he wanted her."

"She's gorgeous," I admitted aloud. "Smart and has her shit together."

"You're smart and have your shit together too."

I rolled my eyes and flopped down on my back. "My shit is not together, at least not yet."

Spencer was definitely distracted by my tits, which were now fully exposed. He tried his hardest to focus only on my face as he swallowed hard.

"I don't like you thinking about yourself that way, babe. How about you spend some time with Mita when we get back to New York?" He started squeezing my nipples, and the sensation streaked down to my pussy.

"Who's Mita?" I asked and then remembered. "Oh right, your therapist." My eyebrows furrowed as I wondered why he would think I needed to see his therapist. "I'll think about it."

Suddenly he sank his warm wet mouth onto my breast. I sucked air as his tongue lapped my nipple.

"You do that," he whispered. "She'll be good for you."

He gently bit the tip, and I gasped and sighed. "Why do you think that?" I asked.

"She'll help you see yourself the way I see you," he said and sank his mouth onto my other breast.

It felt so good, and I knew there would be no

stopping us now. Spencer could never resist it when my breasts flopped enticingly before his eyes. Next his mouth would find its way to my pussy. His tongue would lap my clit. He would stimulate the same tiny spot until I exploded with orgasm and then he'd find another spot and do it again and again, and many more times.

At some point, we would kiss some more. Our making out would turn hot and heavy. As the sun found its way back to our side of the earth, I would become more famished for the hills and hardness of his body. I would kiss him on his chest. He would wince as I bit his nipple. He'd like the way it felt so I'd do it again and again, and then horny as hell and energized by desire like I never felt, I'd run my tongue down his stomach until his solid manhood was in my mouth.

My heartbeat raced, and I felt a drumming in my chest as his thickness stretched my mouth and my tongue slid up and down his shaft. Spencer kept his head pressed against the pillow and his hands on the back of my head as I sucked him. My tongue rounded the tip of his dick and then I took him deeper into my mouth. The sound of him sucking air, moaning, and repeating that he felt it, made me suck harder and take him in deeper. I gave him more and more of what he was wanting and brought him so far down my throat that I felt I would choke.

His body shivered and stiffened and then he shouted, "Oh!"

Warm, salty liquid blasted in my mouth. I wanted and needed him so much that I drank every bit of him. I loved Spencer. I wanted to carry him down my throat and in my belly. I wanted his milk to nourish my cells.

AT SOME POINT WE SLEPT. I WOKE UP TO THE SOUND of my phone ringing on the nightstand. When I reached out to retrieve it, Spencer was still snoring.

I looked at the name on the screen and answered the call.

"Hope, hi?" I whispered, rubbing my eyes.

"Are you just waking up?"

My head was still drowsy. "Yeah..." I sat up against the headboard. "What's up?"

"I'll make it quick. Perry and I are eloping in Vegas, and I want you to be there. Could you come?"

I looked at Spencer, who was waking up.

"When?" I asked.

"Tomorrow night."

Spencer was blinking his way into consciousness. I wasn't sure what his plans were, but suddenly I was haunted by what Jimmy had said about guys like Spencer wanting his woman's pussy accessible whenever he wanted it.

"I'll be there," I said.

"You'll be where?" Spencer whispered.

"Hope and Perry eloping," I whispered as if I was helping them keep the secret. "She wants me there tomorrow, in Vegas."

Spencer rubbed my thigh. I knew exactly what he wanted. "We'll be there," he said. "Oh, and tell her to tell Perry I said congratulations."

"I heard him," Hope said. "I'll relay his message to Perry, and um, remember what I said about those orgasms. Don't ever share that with another woman, not even the maid."

I laughed and told her I loved her and I'd see her tomorrow night.

"You better," she said. "I'll text you the details."

As soon as I put the phone down, Spencer guided me onto my back by my thigh. With my legs spread and pussy screaming for him, a voice blared throughout our room.

"Spence, come join us at the table," Jasper said. "We want to sit down and have a proper meal with you and Jada before we fly back to New York."

That was it.

Spencer and I widened our eyes at each other.

"He's demanding," I said, grinning.

"That's my brother for ya," he said and finished what he started.

Spencer did exactly what Hope had warned me to keep to myself. After my body stiffened and I cried out in pure ecstasy, we both went to our separate bathrooms to dress. We decided to not meet each other in the main sitting area. Since Spencer would naturally be ready before me, he would go down to the table and I would arrive after him.

I showered and put on one of the pretty dresses Lourdes had given me. I was more secure about hanging around Holly Christmas than I had been yesterday. Spencer and Hope had helped me see the light. As I studied myself in the mirror, my hair cascading over my shoulders and a dust of makeup on my face that made me look naturally pretty, I asked myself a surprising question.

"Maybe I should," I whispered, answering myself. Maybe I should sit with Spencer's therapist and really talk about how to move forward living without my mom in my life. I couldn't cut her out. That was for sure. I would never be able to trust her either. I felt as if there was another option that involved accepting things the way they were without allowing my mother to pull me down into her dark and bottomless vortex.

"I'll do it," I whispered and pranced confidently out of the bathroom.

"Hey," Spencer said before I reached the door.

I whipped my face in his direction. "I thought…"

He was approaching me fast. My heart was on edge and then his lips were on mine. His fingers sneaked through the crotch of my panties, his tongue and fingers pushing deeper inside me.

———

"WHAT THE HELL, SPENCE?" JASPER SAID, throwing his hands up. "Why did it take you so long?"

When Jane saw me, she pumped her arms excitedly and said, "Jaja…"

Holly's face lit up as she gasped. "Oh, my God, Jasper, she said Jada!"

I think it was the pure excitement on Holly's

face that made me love her. I sat beside Holly and Jane and told Holly about our adventures in the swimming pool and then our walk around the property yesterday. September and I had had a fun time pushing an excited Jane across the pool on all the toys and teaching her to swim. After eating grilled hot dogs, potato salad, and chips, we had all gone on a walk, *ooh*ing and *ahh*ing at all the picturesque views the property had to offer.

"You, Jane, and I have to get together and do that with each other soon," Holly said and then the sides of her mouth turned downward. "I hate I missed it."

When Jane saw her mother's sad face, she pressed both hands on Holly's cheeks and kissed her lips, comforting her. That one act gave me a bout of illumination. The mother was sad and the daughter made her happy. Shit, I had been living my life wanting and dreading the innate drive to make my mother happy.

"So, Spencer," I said. "I'm going to see Mita."

He smiled as he nodded.

We talked about Holly's plan to head to the evidence locker later that day. She was taking Jane with her, and a BCN television crew was going to meet her there to take video of the evidence, including the van Charlotte had used to escape the compound. It had been parked in Spencer's mother's detached garage for the past thirteen years, and before that it was in Portland, Maine. The two women had been afraid to turn-over the evidence but knew the day would come when they would be able to not only tell their story but assist in making those who harmed them pay.

They didn't want to get too deep into a conversation about the horrid events Charlotte and Irina had suffered because Jane was at the table, but Holly said that both women would soon appear on a special segment with her on the Rochester Report.

"Their story is just remarkable," Holly said. "And Charlotte is…" She closed her eyes and shook her head as if she were tasting something delicious. Then she widened her eyes at Spencer. "And, Spencer, she's your mother for goodness' sake. You came from her."

Spencer gazed at the table, smiling, and then he looked at me.

If only he were sitting next to me. I would've kissed him, but I nodded, smiling at him.

He tilted his head to the side, gesturing for me to sit next to him. I kissed Jane on her rosy little cheek and then took the seat beside him.

Brunch was served, and we all talked for hours. We talked about my mother and everything Jasper and Spencer knew about her.

"There are whispers that she's going to run for president," Jasper said.

"No way," I said, shaking my head adamantly. "My mother wants to be in politics for life. A president has eight years and then that's it. So, I guarantee that's not true. But—" I raised a finger emphatically. "I've been trying to get Spencer to challenge her for her senate seat."

Jasper jerked his head backward. "That's a good idea, Spence. You are still a California resident. Take her on while you're ebbing high."

"No," Spencer said, shaking his head continuously. "Absolutely not."

"No…" a small voice said. "Do, do, dupey, ot," Jane repeated.

We all laughed, and Holly's eyes and mouth expanded again. "You see," she said. "This is why Jasper and I have curbed our bad words."

"Bad woods," Jane repeated.

We all burst with laughter again.

"Excuse me," a short man in khaki shorts and a shirt with his name tag on his chest said.

"What is it, Joe?" Jasper asked.

"There someone here to see Jada Forte. A man. His name is Jim Lovell."

"Oh, sh—" I said, stopping myself before I finished saying shit.

"What the fuck," Spencer blurted and then looked at Jane, knowing he'd screwed up.

Thank goodness she didn't repeat that.

Spencer hopped to his feet. "I'll handle it."

I stood. "I forgot to tell you."

"Tell me what?" he snapped.

"He said he had something on my mother. I told him he'd have to tell me what it was later because I was in Phoenix. The news reports about the evidence clued him that I was with you, and now here he is."

Spencer pointed his palm at me. "Just sit, Jada. I'll deal with Jimmy. I don't want you seeing him."

My neck jutted forward. I felt uncomfortable with Spencer trying to order me around. When I looked at Holly, she raised her eyebrows at me in a way that Hope certainly would've after witnessing what Spencer had just said to me.

I put both my hands on Spencer's strong chest. "Babe, let's keep Controlling Spencer Ken Doll in the box."

He narrowed an eye thoughtfully.

"Ooh," Holly said. "I like that. I'm going to use it when it's time to keep Controlling Jasper Ken Doll in the box too."

Finally, Spencer rolled his eyes. "Babe, he just can't show up at another man's house to speak to his... girlfriend." It sounded as if it killed him to have to call me his girlfriend and not something like his fiancée or wife.

I nodded understandably. "Listen, I know Jimmy is all about crossing boundaries if it benefits him, and everything in the world is supposed to benefit him in his tiny bird brain. But I want to hear what he has to say about Mom. So let's go talk to him together, okay?"

Spencer smashed his lips together as his eyebrows ruffled. I patiently gave him a moment to think. When he finally nodded, I kissed him gently on the lips.

"Kiss," Jane said.

We both looked at her in awe.

"REALLY?" JIMMY ASKED WITH HIS HANDS UP. "YOU can't invite me up to the house?"

Spencer and I had taken a golf cart down to the gate.

"No," Spencer said as he stepped out from behind the wheel.

"Jada, come on, I asked for you, not him." Jimmy was beet red and clearly pissed that Spencer was with me. He had a frown pasted on his face, and Jimmy was generally a smirker more than he was a frowner.

"Whatever you have to say to her, you can say to me," Spencer said, now standing only a few feet away from Jimmy.

Jimmy pushed his hand at us. "You know what? Fuck it. I'm keeping it to myself." He turned his back on us and took steps toward a huge Jeep, which I assumed was his rental car.

"Jimmy?" I called after him, and he stopped in his tracks.

Spencer grunted, letting me know he was unhappy about how quickly Jimmy had responded to me.

I expanded my eyes at Spencer. "Spencer, please be nice."

Now he threw his hands up.

Jimmy turned to face us and then folded his arms across his chest. "I only want to talk to you."

"Spencer and I are a duo, Jimmy. Come on, I heard my mother may be running for president. Is that true?"

Jimmy pressed his lips. However, he hadn't turned his back on me, and I took it as a good sign.

"If she's running for president, then that means she believes she's in the clear regarding the illegal donations to her campaign. Not to mention she's gotten away with having herself shot and then trying to blame it on my brother."

Jimmy shook his head as if he was stunned by what I just said. "She did that?"

I nodded enthusiastically. "Yes, she did."

He stood very still as he turned to gaze off, then after a forceful sigh, he said, "She and I have been fucking."

My mouth fell open, and I had to keep my legs from collapsing. "What?"

"I have proof that she was using me. Do you want it?"

I was still speechless.

"We want it," Spencer said decidedly.

A small cunning smile etched its way onto Jimmy's lips, and that's when I knew he had planned all of this. It wasn't me he came here looking for. It was Spencer. Only, he knew Spencer would never give him the time of day.

"You fucking parasite," I said, shaking my head.

"I want you to clear me and my family from the list of those who were taking those donations. I only opened accounts in my families' names because of Patricia. And she found a way to clear her name."

I'd seen many facets of Jimmy in the short time I had worked for him but never that vulnerable and pleading look on his face. Spencer's scowl remained just as intense regardless. He had no empathy for Jimmy.

"What's your proof?" Spencer asked.

Jimmy gazed at me and then at Spencer. After a moment, he took his phone out of his pocket and looked at me. "Do you still have the same email address?"

I cleared the frog out of my throat. "I do, but my phone is in the house."

Spencer kept his glare on Jimmy. "Babe, would you take the golf cart and go get it?"

"I will," I whispered.

"You two really are together, huh?" Jimmy asked.

Spencer's glare deepened. I wasn't going to answer that question. It was the least I could do to not irritate my future fiancé. I was determined to say yes the next time he asked me to be his wife.

I drove up to the house, went to the bedroom, and got my phone. Jimmy requested to AirDrop several videos to my phone. I accepted his request. I couldn't wait until I reached Spencer to see what was contained in them.

I drew my face up as I watched Jimmy bang my mother. What I was watching was disgusting yet intriguing. "Holy shit," I muttered.

Then, I received an email from Jimmy that said: "I would've rather it been you."

I clutched my stomach and swallowed to keep myself from throwing up.

SPENCER, JASPER, HOLLY, AND I HAD WATCHED ALL of Jimmy's recordings together. He had my mom on camera reminding him that he was nothing but her "hard dick and hired help."

Jane was upstairs with September so we could all curse freely.

"What the fuck is wrong with her?" I asked.

"She's sick on power." Jasper had the exact same intense look on his face that Spencer did.

"Spence, she has to be handled," Jasper said, purposely avoiding looking at me.

"But she's Jada's mother. So you guys have to consider that," Holly said.

"No," I said quickly. "It's fine. My mother can fight her own battles. She's counting on me to keep the Christmases from nailing her ass to the wall. I'm not on her side." I swallowed hard and then nodded emphatically. "Nail her."

Spencer narrowed his eyes at me. I knew my words had gotten him hot and bothered and he wanted to fuck me silly.

Jasper, on the other hand, seemed to take what I had said as a green light to go get her. He nodded curtly. "Done."

CHAPTER FIFTEEN

JADA FORTE

After our long brunch, Spencer and I flew to Las Vegas and then later Jasper and Holly would fly to New York. Our flight was shorter, but Spencer and I were spending every second of it in bed. His hands were clasped around my waist, our bodies tense after he'd just nailed me with his final thrust. We both shivered as our moans rang out in unison and then Spencer drew me against him. Neither of us minded the heat and sweat emanating from both our bodies.

Usually when we were making love, my mind was a hundred percent in the action, but this time it wasn't. I couldn't stop thinking about Jasper and Spencer vowing to "handle" my mother and how I had zealously agreed. It wasn't that I was having

205

second thoughts. I was worried about what she would do to Spencer. I was the only reason she hadn't chosen to annihilate him. I was sure of it.

Spencer kissed the hot spot on the back of my shoulder, and I shivered. Of course, he did it again, and I had the same reaction. Then he reached around my pelvis to roll the tip of his finger around my clit. He liked it when I was all hot and bothered and horny, even if his cock was out of steam.

"Spencer," I said with a sigh.

"Yeah, baby," he replied breathlessly.

I forced myself to not concentrate on the sensations beginning to flicker in my pussy. "I don't think I ever told you that my mom has a video with you in St. Barthes. It seems Jimmy is quite the videographer."

He stopped stimulating me cold turkey.

"What are you talking about?" he asked, the lustful haze scrubbed from his tone.

"To prove that you were a horrible guy and a woman-beater, she had Jimmy play me a video of you at a party with Gina. Her face was battered, and you were wrangling her back into the bedroom."

"I'm not a woman-beater," he said.

I kissed his solid bicep. "Of course you're not,

babe. But my mom is going to create her own narrative."

"I don't fucking care what narrative she creates. Gina and I know the truth. We were both fucking sick."

"I know," I whispered and then another thought came to mind. "I can get you through any accusations she throws your way." I shimmied around to face him.

Spencer looked as if he were chewing on lemons. His expression told me that he indeed cared about my mom attempting to sully his reputation.

"I can be your PR manager."

"Okay," he said without pause.

I smirked. "That's it? I don't have to interview for the job?"

"You've been interviewing since I first met you."

We kissed, just as the pilot announced that we should prepare for landing. This time we actually got out of bed and took a quick shower together, focusing on cleaning ourselves and not making out and putting our mouths and fingers in other places. Then we dressed and strapped ourselves into the front cabin seats for landing.

Las Vegas was warmer than Phoenix. It was late afternoon. Hope and Perry weren't scheduled to arrive until tomorrow morning. I'd been sitting in the back seat of our hired car for the past twenty minutes, waiting for Spencer. Soon after we had landed, he received a call from his investigator, then his brother and finally his mother, who was actually calling him more on an official level than a personal one.

I felt as if Spencer hadn't spoken enough about Charlotte Wright to me. He was the sort who took longer than the average person to process things. Spencer needed to understand situations and people on a deeper level than most. I figured he was still captured by the phase of surprise and disbelief. However, he had closed me into the back seat of the car and stepped away when he was speaking to her. I wished he wouldn't have because I was curious to hear their conversation.

Arthur Valentine had been arrested and was being held without bail. Irina and Charlotte's stories had been released to all worldwide press outlets. Some had already picked up the story in their late editions of the news. The twenty-four-hour news cycle was going crazy with the story, and Nestor had warned us to keep a low profile until Spencer was able to give an official interview on BCN. He had promised to give his sister-in-law the interview, who professionally went by Holly Henderson. I learned during brunch that Christmas Industries owned the station, which meant Jasper and Spencer had more power than Superman.

I sighed with relief when I caught sight of Spencer gaiting toward the car. I expected him to get in on the other side, but instead he opened my door and held out his hand for me to take.

Confused, I stepped my feet on the concrete and got out of the car. "What is it?"

"Our car has been identified by reporters. I'm driving us."

I tried to ignore the fact that he looked irritated, despite all the good news he'd received about Valentine being locked up, and I wondered if his foul mood had anything to do with the conversation with his mother.

We were driven in one of those carts that airport workers use to get around the field to an office building where there was no one around. Spencer kept hold of my hand as we walked through a hallway and out a door where a small gray midsized sedan was parked.

I couldn't help but grin when I saw the car. "Is that what you're driving?"

He smirked. "What? You don't think I know how to drive an ordinary car?"

I chuckled. "No. Not really."

Spencer trotted ahead of me a few steps and opened the door. He caught me by the waist before I got in and I gazed into his smoldering eyes.

"I guess I have to show you that I'm a man of all trades."

I couldn't help myself. I knotted my arms around his neck and initiated a head-spinning smooch. The seconds whizzed by as our lips and tongues delicately slid against each other. There was no drug better than kissing Spencer Christmas. If I could bottle our kiss and sell it, I'd be an instant billionaire too.

"I love you, baby," he finally whispered.

"I love you too," I said without a shadow of a doubt.

I knew I could never live without him, ever.

Spencer seemed out of place behind the wheel of an average car. Perhaps it was because I associated him with the sort of opulence that was out-of-this-world ritzy. It was the way he walked, talked, tasted, even smelled that told the story of how rich he was. From the ranch to his private airplane, to his penthouse in Manhattan, then the mansion in

Scottsdale—and not to mention all of his servants —Spencer lived above typical.

"So where are we going?" I asked.

"Somewhere quiet, off the Strip."

"Oh," I said.

I glanced at Spencer, who had pressed his lips. We usually had more to say to each other, but he seemed a little tense.

"How was your conversation with your mother?" I asked, figuring that could give me some answers about his current mood.

"It was fine."

"Why did she call?"

His jaw became tighter. "Just checking in."

I felt my eyebrows furrow. Spencer was certainly being secretive again.

Suddenly he reached out to take my hand. "Hey, let's just relax and not think about any of the shit that's been going on in the past couple of days." He glanced at me and then put his eyes back on the road. "Okay?"

I twisted my mouth thoughtfully. I wonder if he'd meant I could really be his PR person. If that was the case, then he couldn't continue to keep certain things from me.

"Babe, please, come on," he said.

Just as I knew him well, it seemed he knew me well.

I sighed with a groan. "All right but don't forget you said I was your new PR manager. And if I'm in charge of your public image, then you can't keep keeping shit from me."

When Spencer glanced at me, he was smirking. "I won't keep keeping shit from you. I promise."

I rolled my eyes and crossed my arms. "Are you mocking me?"

He shook his head in disbelief. "No, Jada. I would never mock you. I just think you're…"

I jerkily turned my head to the side. "You just think I'm what?"

"Tired, babe. Exhausted."

"I'm no more exhausted than you are." Holy shit, what was wrong with me? I wanted to argue and didn't know why.

"You're right," Spencer said, looking ahead.

Finally, I closed my tired eyes to sigh. "No, you're right. I guess I feel as if you're keeping something from me, and I thought we were beyond secrets."

To my surprise, Spencer didn't say anything. He kept looking straight ahead. The car remained thoughtfully silent until he turned into a parking lot of a helicopter airfield.

"Are we going to get on one of those?" I asked.

"Yes," he said as he stopped in front of the hangar's front entrance and turned off the car.

I knew how voracious the press could be, and with all that was going on, I figured Spencer had to take some unique steps to outsmart them.

"Well, where are we staying tonight?" I asked.

He winked at me with his mouth-watering smirk. "I'll show you, come on."

He hopped out of the car before I could respond.

Spencer opened my door and took my hand. My legs felt wobbly as we entered the building. I felt my eyes expand when I saw a man, wearing a black suit, standing behind a table that had an assortment of rings on top of it.

Suddenly Spencer dropped on his knee in front of me. My neck jutted forward, and my mouth fell open.

"Jada Forte, will you marry me?" he asked.

My shocked gaze shifted from the table with the rings to the man I loved kneeling before me. I sure as hell wasn't going get it wrong this time.

I narrowed an eye, making an exaggerated angry face. "I knew you were keeping a secret."

He took my hand and kissed the back of it.

His touch nearly took my breath away as I got down on my knees to join him.

Spencer leaned back, surprised.

I took his face in my hands. "Babe, I'll marry you a million times in a million lifetimes if that's how many times you asked me."

Our mouths melted together, and we rolled around on the hard and highly glossed floor, kissing and not caring who saw us. Finally, he got me on my back and straddled himself above me.

"Will you marry me now?" he asked.

My eyes expanded. "Now?"

I heard clapping and then people he and I knew started walking into the main room from hallways. I saw Bryn of all people, Jasper, Holly, and little Jane, our parrot. I slapped a hand over my mouth and gasped when Hope ran toward me. Spencer lifted me off the floor before she reached me, and when she arrived, we hugged each other long and hard. My other girlfriends were here too—Rita, Ling, Porsha, Mavis, and Angela and their dates. I saw Perry and narrowed my eyes at him.

"Aren't you guys getting married tomorrow?" I asked Hope.

"Hell no," she said. "Old Money Mama has won the battle, but she won't win the fucking war." She turned to look over her shoulder at Perry. "Right, sweetheart?"

Perry showed her a thumbs-up.

Spencer whipped me over to the table to have me pick out my ring. There was one that stood out from the other over-encrusted diamond rings. This one was a silver band with one sparkling diamond. The simplicity took my breath away. I took it out of the velvet slot and put on my finger. It fit perfectly.

I smiled up at Spencer who was standing beside me. "You knew I would choose this, didn't you?"

He winked at me, and everyone clapped as we kissed.

With my head spinning, as it usually did when I kissed Spencer, I asked, "Are we getting married here?"

He turned his head slightly. "Babe, come on. The ring is you, but the wedding is all me. And there's someone else I want you to meet." He waved over a woman with short hair and a beautiful but hardened face.

"It's my mother," he said to me, eyes gleaming.

Then he said it louder for everyone to hear. "It's my mother."

Guests clapped as I hugged Charlotte Wright.

Charlotte congratulated me and said she couldn't wait to spend more time with us.

"But hey," she said, still holding my hands. "Let's not waste any more time. You two get ready to get married."

The room erupted in applause and cheers.

Hope hooked her arm around mine and started pulling me away from Spencer. "Time to say goodbye to Prince Charming." She cupped a hand around the side of her mouth as she whispered, "With a golden dick," in my ear.

I rolled my eyes as I let her lead me away. I watched Jasper and Perry pull Spencer in a different direction. We both reached out for each other playfully as we parted in such sweet sorrow.

HOPE HAD BEEN PART OF THE DRESS-FINDING mission. All my friends including Holly, who was my new friend and would soon officially be my sister-in-law, gathered in a room that seemed to be designed just for me. For sure the white sofas surrounding a rack with ten wedding dresses on it was not the normal décor. I loved them all, but I settled on a simple spaghetti-strapped white dress with a plunging neckline that made my cleavage look delicious.

"How do you feel about Patricia not being here?" Hope asked as she zipped me up.

The faces in the room were sympathetic. It wasn't as if they didn't know my mom and I were on the outs. All they had to do was watch the news and then call Hope and ask how I was doing. They all knew how volatile my relationship had always been with my mother. Hope would've told them Patricia and I weren't in a good place, and my friends would've left it at that. But just thinking of my mom not being a part of my wedding day made tears pool in my eyes. However, I would not let them fall, not on the day when I would officially be Mrs. Jada Anne Christmas.

I swallowed my gloom and shrugged. "I just wish my dad was here. That's all."

Hope grunted thoughtfully as her eyebrows lifted.

I gasped as I slapped a hand over my heart. "He's here?"

She hooked her arm around mine and told all the women to follow her.

My father stood at the end of the hallway, and when I saw him, I ripped my arm out of my friendship link with Hope and ran to embrace my dad.

ALL THE MEN EXCEPT MY DAD WERE GONE. THE rest of us filed into six helicopters that took off one by one, parading through the sky one behind the other. We eventually landed in a valley, high in the plains of Red Rock Canyon. Our wedding location was set with white chairs and a large canopy, catering with full service, a dance floor, and a complete orchestra.

As soon as I stepped out of the helicopter, the wedding march must've begun. When the aircraft pulled away, I heard it continue to resonate softly through the air. Spencer, now dressed in a suit, watched me in awe as I headed toward him with my dad by my side. Holy shit, this was finally happening. Spencer and I would soon be husband and wife.

Twenty-Three Hours Later

"Ah!" I cried out from a penthouse condo high above the Las Vegas Strip.

Spencer and I had gotten zero sleep after our wedding, which had been a blast. We danced, ate, and laughed to our hearts' content. Then when we arrived at Spencer's place, we fucked, made love, I blew him, he went down on me, and we did it over and over again. Now that we were husband and wife, and so excited about it, Spencer's dick had a new kind of stamina. Twenty minutes after coming and he was up again and ready to go.

After his cock of gold stimulated me to climax, he shivered against me, releasing his nectar. His hands were cupping my tits, squeezing my nipples, informing me that there would be another round within twenty minutes and not to even think about falling asleep.

"Shit, baby," he said with his mouth against my ear before his tongue dove into the canal. "I can't get enough of you."

I chuckled. "What's new?"

He nailed me with his soft cock. "You're going to pay for that pretty soon."

I flipped on my back to face him. "I can't wait."

Before our lips could connect, Spencer's phone announced that Jasper was calling.

We both knew Jasper's wasn't a call Spencer ignored. He snatched his device off the nightstand and answered it.

"Hello," Spencer said.

The more Jasper spoke, the more intense Spencer's frown turned.

"What?" he finally said and then turned on the TV.

Spencer flicked the channels until he landed on BCN.

"I'm there," Spencer said and then, after a moment, he ended their call.

"What is it?" I asked.

Spencer reached out to guide me against him. "It's your mother. BCN is going to replay an interview she'd done after the commercials."

I closed my eyes and took a deep, steadying breath. Of course she had found out about the wedding and that she hadn't been invited. Knowing my mom, that meant war and the fight was on.

The commercial ended, and Spencer held me

closer as an anchor named Crystal Carter started with an introduction to the clip.

"Senator Forte has claimed that the Christmas family has started a feud with her simply because she didn't agree with her daughter marrying the sought-after bachelor Spencer Hunter Christmas."

A clip of my mother filled our screen. She was walking down the steps at the state capitol building in California as reporters were following her.

At first she spoke on the shooter not being found but that her security believed it was a botched attempted robbery. Then one of them asked about Spencer's and my recent marriage.

"He has my daughter brainwashed. He's a Christmas of course, and we know how diabolical the father was, and the sons are too."

"Senator, are you saying that Spencer Christmas will harm your daughter?"

She shrugged indifferently. "He lied when he turned my name in to the FBI. I'm sure he'll lie again. I say watch out for him. That's enough."

"What about running for president?" a reporter asked.

"Let's win one race at a time," she said.

They yelled after her with more questions. Spencer turned off the TV. Anger settled around us as we both sat against the backboard, staring at the blank screen.

"Now would you do it?" I asked. "Beat her in her own district?"

Spencer continued glaring at the television as if the hate in his eyes would soon set it on fire. "Yes."

I jerked my head backward, thinking perhaps I'd heard him wrong. "Did you say yes?"

He turned toward me. "If you're serious, then I'm serious."

My eyes expanded. "Oh, I'm serious."

"Then let's do it."

First, we shook on it. The longer we looked into each other's eyes led us to kiss on it. Next, he was inside me. Soon we would sleep, and when we woke up, we'd be ready for war.

Spencer and Jada's war against Patricia Forte in *Exposed, Boss Billionaire Spencer Christmas*.

Made in the USA
San Bernardino, CA
16 June 2020

73409311R00126